"You can let me go now, Sterne," Brynn said with steely determination.

She slipped her bare foot on top of his and ground her heel into his toes to add emphasis to her request.

"But I love holding you, sweetheart." Sterne hissed in pain as she continued to mash his foot with the force of one stomping grapes. In retaliation, he bent his head and nipped the sensitive skin of her neck. Then he began to lick.

His sensual retaliation was alarmingly, instantly effective. Brynn reacted as if she'd been struck by lightning. She removed her foot from his and drew in her breath in a startled gasp. She was suddenly, intensely aware of the size and strength of the man holding her, of the heat of his hard body. She felt his lips and his teeth and his tongue on her neck, and sharp tendrils of sexual excitement uncurled in her abdomen.

For one crazy moment, she felt an overwhelming urge to close her eyes and surrender to the man who held her, to the delicious sensations that tempted her toward the edge. . . .

WHAT ARE *LOVESWEPT* ROMANCES?

They are stories of true romance and touching emotion. We believe those two very important ingredients are constants in our highly sensual and very believable stories in the *LOVESWEPT* line. Our goal is to give you, the reader, stories of consistently high quality that may sometimes make you laugh, sometimes make you cry, but are always fresh and creative and contain many delightful surprises within their pages.

Most romance fans read an enormous number of books. Those they truly love, they keep. Others may be traded with friends and soon forgotten. We hope that each *LOVESWEPT* romance will be a treasure—a "keeper." We will always try to publish

LOVE STORIES YOU'LL NEVER FORGET
BY AUTHORS YOU'LL ALWAYS REMEMBER

The Editors

LOVESWEPT® • 194

Barbara Boswell
Not a Marrying Man

 BANTAM BOOKS
TORONTO • NEW YORK • LONDON • SYDNEY • AUCKLAND

NOT A MARRYING MAN

A Bantam Book / June 1987

If you would be interested in receiving protective vinyl covers for your Loveswept books, please write to this address for information:

Loveswept
Bantam Books
P.O. Box 985
Hicksville, NY 11802

ISBN 0-553-21829-8

Published simultaneously in the United States and Canada

PRINTED IN THE UNITED STATES OF AMERICA

O   0 9 8 7 6 5 4 3 2 1

One

Sterne Lipton was bored. He held a double martini—fixed exactly the way he liked it—and sipped it indifferently as he surveyed the well-dressed crowd. They were all mingling in the spacious terraced gardens surrounding the elegant home of the party's host and hostess, Douglas and Violet Kaye. It was a warm June night, a full moon shone brilliantly in the black velvet sky, and the fragrances of dozens of varieties of flowers and shrubs sweetened the air.

All of Washington D.C.'s young movers and shakers were present and accounted for, along with a flock of beautiful young women and men who'd been invited to serve as decoration and entertainment for those guests whose presence *really* counted.

Sterne knew that as President Bradford Lipton's eldest son, he was considered one of those who *really* counted. He was the extra bachelor that all the Washington hostesses wanted for their tables. He was the dashing man-about-town that all those pretty little girls fresh from college wanted to date. And the career women, from their late twenties to their early forties, the ones who'd been in Washington for years and had worked their way up to positions of power and respect? They wanted him too. For dates, for their tables, for their beds.

He had it made, Sterne acknowledged to himself. At thirty-four, he was a self-professed rake in a rake's paradise. Women were at his beck and call. Women were eager to please him, in whatever ways he chose to be pleased.

And he was bored. During the past year he'd slipped from a vague dissatisfaction to an almost overwhelming ennui. All the usual pleasures—sex, food, drink, music, travel—everything seemed to have lost its luster.

"Doug and Vi really know how to throw a party, hey, Sterne?"

Sterne glanced at the blond-haired, blue-eyed Adonis who'd joined him at his stakeout position along the stone wall of the garden. He was Chad Chambers, son of the liberal senator from New York. Bradford Lipton had defeated Senator Chambers for the party's presidential nomination two years ago. Sterne and Chad, both "political brats" who had grown up in Washington as sons of politically prominent fathers, had known each other for years.

Sterne shrugged. "Yeah."

"This is Kyle Zimmer, my father's new media consultant," Chad continued. For the first time, Sterne noticed the shorter blond man standing beside Chad. "Kyle, Sterne Lipton."

Kyle Zimmer didn't seem to be particularly impressed at meeting the President's son. He merely nodded, his light blue eyes fixed on the party guests dancing on the wide flagstone patio.

"She's the one," Zimmer muttered, presumably to Chad although Sterne was clearly within earshot. "The sexy redhead. I've had my eye on her since I got here an hour ago. It's time to make my move."

Both Chad and Sterne's gazes followed Kyle Zimmer's

to a young auburn-haired woman. She was wearing a silky emerald-colored dress and laughing and flirting with her partner on the outdoor dance floor.

"That's Brynnie!" Sterne exclaimed.

"You know her?" Zimmer asked, glancing at Sterne. "Introduce me to her, Lipton."

"She's my little sister's best friend." Sterne continued to stare at Brynn Cassidy, who seemed to be thoroughly enjoying the dance with her dark-haired, dark-eyed partner. Brynn was typically exuberant, energetic, and animated. She always had been. But sexy? Little Brynnie? Sterne's brows drew together. "I've known her for fifteen years, since she and Stacey were twelve. Brynn's like a kid sister to me."

"Well, my feelings for the lady are not in the least brotherly." Zimmer smiled, displaying his even white teeth. "Are you going to introduce me to her, Lipton, or shall I do it myself?"

Sterne glanced from Zimmer to Brynn. He didn't care for the look in Zimmer's eye; he'd felt it in his own often enough. It was the predatory look of a wolf stalking its prey, the sexual confidence of a male who did not intend to spend the night alone.

"Find yourself another playmate, Zimmer," Sterne growled. "Brynnie's not that kind of girl."

Chad Chambers snickered. "What Sterne means is that he's never gotten anywhere with Brynn Cassidy. And neither have I," he added wryly. "I dated her a few years ago and struck out cold."

"If she rejected you two," Zimmer said with a smug smile, "she's obviously a woman of taste and discrimination. *I'll* have no trouble getting whatever I want from her."

Sterne scowled. He didn't like the idea of this blond hotshot getting whatever he wanted from little Brynnie.

"Brynn's never rejected me," Sterne said. "I've never even come close to making a pass at her. Why would I? I've already told you we have a brother-sister relationship."

"She'd choose me even if you were to make a pass at her, Lipton," Zimmer said with maddening confidence. "You can bet on it."

Sterne eyed him coldly. "If you don't shut up, I may just take you up on that bet, Zimmer. And senators' aides need to watch their pennies, don't they?"

"Unlike you spoiled rich boys with your trust funds and your potential inheritances, I do have to be careful with my money," Zimmer retorted.

"Sterne doesn't live off his family," Chad said in a surprising display of loyalty. "He's a working stiff— proprietor of Sterne's Place in Georgetown and Sterne's Place Two in Rehoboth Beach."

Zimmer's smile was closer to a sneer. "Oh, sure, those sleazy meat markets. If you weren't packing in the tourists hoping to catch a glimpse of the President's notorious son, those dives would've closed long ago."

Sterne didn't rise to the bait. What Zimmer said was probably true. He'd opened the singles' bars nearly five years ago, deliberately cultivating a meat-market image. They'd been moderately successful, but business had been fading until his father won the presidency. Suddenly both Sterne's places were booming—and curious tourists did seem to make up the bulk of the crowd. Sterne didn't particularly care who patronized his bars; he spent less and less time there. He was bored with them both.

"Are you interested in making a bet?" Chad pressed, as if determined to evoke some sort of reaction from Sterne.

Sterne shrugged laconically. He rarely expended emotion. Sometimes he wondered if he were capable of doing so.

"May I suggest the stakes?" Chad continued when Sterne failed to reply. "If Zimmer get Brynn Cassidy into bed within the month, Lipton has to pay him a h⸻dred dollars. And vice versa, of course."

⸻rne smiled a sudden crocodilian smile. "Let's make

the time limit two weeks and the money one thousand dollars." He had the satisfaction of seeing Kyle Zimmer look thoroughly disconcerted.

"Can't meet the terms, Zimmer?" Sterne asked, regarding him with mild amusement. "Perhaps you'd better reconsider, Chambers. Your man doesn't seem like such a sure win, after all, hmm?"

"I have every confidence in Kyle," Chad said heartily, slapping Zimmer on the back. "He's a winner."

After such a vote of confidence, what could the man say? Kyle Zimmer squared his shoulders and met Sterne's gaze. "You're on, Lipton. I accept the terms and I'm going to win."

"Terrific!" Chad rubbed his hands together gleefully. I want in on this. I'm betting five hundred bucks that Zimmer will beat you out with Brynn Cassidy, Sterne."

"That means you'll have to pay me five hundred when Zimmer loses, Chad," Sterne reminded him.

Chad shrugged. "Money is no object." He, too, had a trust fund and old family money behind him.

Sterne smiled. "Collecting from you two boneheads is going to be a rare pleasure."

"Just remember, you don't collect unless you score," Chad said. "Having Kyle strike out isn't enough. You have to get the girl into bed within two weeks or you lose."

"Piece of cake," Sterne said with an indifferent shrug.

Kyle Zimmer muttered something under his breath about spoiled rich boys and lessons to be learned, then stalked away without a backward glance. Sterne watched him weave his way through the dancers to Brynn's side, and cut in on Brynn's partner.

"Looks like Zimmer is making his way to the inside track with her," Chad said eagerly.

"Not if I have anything to say about it," Sterne muttered. For the first time in a long while, he was roused from his usual state of apathy. This was Brynnie they were talking about, for Pete's sake. He knew her as well as he knew his own sister. Which wasn't to say he was close to either Stacey or Brynn. He was, by choice, close to no one. Still, he had a certain fondness for Brynn. Like his sister, she'd been on the periphery of his life for a long time.

"Brynn's a sweet kid," Sterne added, frowning. "Let that blond shark find someone else to play with." Impulsively, he started through the crowd.

"Forget it, Sterne," Chad called after him with a hoot of laughter. "I'm not buying the white knight routine and Brynn won't either. There's not a chivalrous bone in your decadent body. You just want to win that bet. Little Miss Cassidy is in more danger from her surrogate big brother Sterne than from any blond shark she'll ever encounter."

"I haven't been able to take my eyes off you since the first moment I saw you this evening," Kyle Zimmer murmured in Brynn Cassidy's ear. His teeth circled her earlobe and she felt the warm breath from his nostrils fan her neck. His hand moved slowly, sensuously over her back as he purposefully thrust the lower half of his body against her hips.

Just in case she wasn't getting his message, Brynn thought dryly. But she was getting it, loud and clear. And she wasn't interested. "I agreed to finish out this dance with you when you cut in, but that doesn't grant you a license to maul me," she said firmly. "If you want a warm body for the night, I suggest you find one of the girls invited specifically for that purpose, Kyle."

He stared at her, momentarily nonplussed. Before he could recover, Sterne Lipton cut in on him. "Excuse me, Zimmer. Brynnie and I are going to dance this one."

With even greater ease than Zimmer had displayed in disposing of Brynn's previous partner, Stern disposed of Zimmer. He swept Brynn deep into the crowd of dancers.

"Do you mind telling me what's going on?" Brynn

asked. "I haven't been in such demand since I won a *piñata* stuffed with candy in the third grade."

"I wanted to dance with you, okay?"

"Not okay. You've known me for fifteen years and you've never felt the urge to dance with me before. Besides, I saw that triumphant leer you flashed at Zimmer."

"Zimmer is an overconfident, obnoxious frog. Stay away from him, Brynnie."

"Uh-oh." She glanced over Sterne's shoulder. "Here comes Froggie—and looking very determined too. Would I be wrong in guessing that he's on his way to grab me from you?"

Sterne looked around and saw Kyle Zimmer grimly threading his way through the dancers, his gaze fixed on Brynn. "You guessed right, honey. Let's get out of here."

Keeping a firm hold on her hand, Sterne dragged Brynn through the crowd, out of the garden, and into the Kayes' brightly lit stone and stucco mansion.

"Sterne, what's this all about?" Brynn asked as she stumbled after him. The skinny heels of her thin-strapped green leather sandals were much too high for the kind of fast walking that Sterne was forcing her to do. "Why are we running away from Kyle Zimmer? Who is he, anyway? What—"

"Violet, great party, darling," Sterne called to their hostess as they passed her en route to the front door. "Yes, we're making an early night of it. Ciao, love."

"Sterne!" Brynn tried to stop as Sterne dragged her out the front door. She refused to move, but Sterne didn't seem to notice. He pulled her forward, jerking her off balance, and she crashed into the hard wall of his back. "Let me go!" She tried and failed to escape from the manaclelike grip he had on her. "Sterne, I can't leave now. I came to the party with a date. He'll be looking for me and—"

"—he won't find you," Sterne finished for her, stopping and turning to look down at her. "You're leaving now, Brynnie. Resign yourself to it."

"What kind of trouble have you gotten yourself into this time?" Brynn demanded crossly. "Why is Zimmer after us? I haven't seen you move so fast since you claimed that female Communist—what was her name? Nadia?—was chasing you at that British Embassy reception for the Eastern bloc countries."

Sterne shuddered. "The woman had the thickest ankles and the broadest shoulders I've ever seen. And she was mad for me. As if I'd ever bed a KGB agent!"

"You didn't object to her being in the KGB, you objected to her thick ankles and broad shoulders," Brynn said succinctly. Her teeth worried her lower lip and she stared at him thoughtfully. "Is Zimmer . . . some sort of agent?"

"Oh, he's an agent, all right. He's Senator Whit Chambers's new media consultant. Blond-haired and blue-eyed, just like Chambers himself. Have you ever noticed that Senator Chambers surrounds himself with blue-eyed blonds? His wife, his kids, his staff. Is that some kind of Aryan ego trip or what?"

Brynn grinned at his indignation. "I think it's heredity that his kids are blond and coincidence that most of his staff is blond."

"You've got all the answers, don't you, little girl?" Sterne paused and stared down into her wide green eyes. She had beautiful eyes, he noticed with some surprise. Large and wide-set and an unusual shade of light green. The color of peridots. And they were surrounded by long, thick black lashes.

He frowned. "Chad Chambers said he used to date you."

"For about a month a few years back," she said.

"He says he got nowhere with you. Why not? Tons of women have fallen for those blond beachboy looks of his. And he has plenty of money and always drives the flashiest cars. . . ."

"And he goes through women the way allergy sufferers go through tissues during ragweed season. Having watched you treat women that same way for years made me totally immune to Chad Chambers's alleged charm. I knew what he was going to say and do before *he* did."

Sterne was somewhat taken aback by her blunt reply. But then, Brynn had always been outspoken. Sometimes she was downright insulting—like the time she'd told him he had the IQ of a clam! Accustomed to being admired for his physique, he'd been totally at a loss when she'd attacked his intellect. So what if he hadn't read a book in years? The more he'd mulled over the insult, the more insulted he'd decided he was. In fact, he became so incensed that he obtained a copy of his IQ test and showed it to her. She'd maintained that the score—in the superior range—was either forged or a misprint.

"Well," she said now, "whatever is going on between you and Zimmer, count me out." Brynn tried once more to pull her hand from Sterne's. He didn't release it. Her impatience began to rise. "Sterne, I really do want to get back to my date."

"Who is your date?"

She rolled her eyes heavenward. "If you must know, his name is Daniel King. He's a senior pediatric resident at Georgetown Hospital and he's a very sweet man."

"A sweet man?" Sterne made a face. "What kind of man is that?"

"The type of man who doesn't see women as objects to be conquered, used, and then blithely tossed aside. The type of man a woman can talk to and depend on. The type of man who is capable of sustaining a relationship with one woman and doesn't run screaming from the word 'commitment.' The type of man who likes children and wants them someday. Shall I go on or do you get the picture?"

"He sounds boring, Brynn."

She laughed. "I'm sure he does—to you. But not to me."

"Are you serious about this guy?"

"This is only our third date," she said thoughtfully. "But I think I could be, Sterne. You know, ever since Stacey married Justin and had the twins, I've been wondering when I would get married. I just adore little Allison and Amanda." She sighed wistfully. "I want so much to have a baby of my own."

"Kindly spare me the feminine mush," Sterne muttered, even as he stared pensively at Brynn's face. Something odd, something undefinable and inexplicable stirred within him. He looked at Brynn and for the first time ever, he saw a woman and not the little girl who'd been his kid sister's constant companion through the years.

She was lovely. High cheekbones and a smooth ivory complexion. Those big, beautiful pale green eyes. A turned-up nose, sprinkled with freckles, and a firm little chin. A well-shaped, generous mouth, now curved in a sweet smile. A face that was always alert and alive with expression and animation.

Sterne was used to making jokes about her redhead's temper, but Brynn's shoulder-length hair wasn't really as much red as a deep auburn, highlighted with blond from the summer sun. It cascaded around her shoulders, the ends curling.

He captured a lock of Brynn's hair and the end curled around his finger. It was a beautiful shade, he realized with something akin to amazement. A glorious combination of copper and gold. And so soft and silky.

Brynn pulled away, annoyed. "Quit messing up my hair, Sterne. If you knew how long it took to get those stupid ends to curl." She frowned, and he knew she was totally, completely unaware of him as anything but the big brother figure he'd been for the past fifteen years.

And he wasn't a big brother figure that she, or even Stacey, particularly admired. Sterne was fully aware of that. Hadn't Brynn once told him that she hoped to marry a man as completely different from him as possible? He had laughed it off, wishing her good luck in her search. He didn't care who she married. As for himself, he was a connoisseur of the proverbial wine, women, and song, and had no intention of settling down.

"Come on, Sterne!" The expression on Brynn's face was growing stormy now. "Give me my hand back. I want to go find Daniel."

"You're not going back in there, Brynn. Zimmer's looking for you."

"So what? I can handle Zimmer."

"He made a bet with Chad Chambers that he could get you into bed within two weeks."

"You're kidding!" Brynn burst out laughing.

"I'm not kidding. There's a lot of money riding on it." For reasons which he didn't care to analyze or examine, Sterne declined to tell her about the other part of the bet, his own part in the wager.

"Do I have to be conscious?" she asked.

"What?"

"When I'm in bed with Zimmer. Does he win the bet if he hits me over the head and puts me into bed before I've regained consciousness?"

"Brynn, I don't think you're taking this as seriously as you should," Sterne said testily.

"How can I take it seriously? It's the most idiotic thing I've ever heard! It's like something *you'd* do! And if Kyle Zimmer doesn't plan to render me unconscious to get me into bed, then I'm perfectly safe; because I could never, ever be swayed by the likes of him. I'm totally immune to predatory wolves on the make, Sterne. After all, I grew up watching you exploit women. Why would I ever let myself fall victim to a shallow, self-centered womanizer?"

"Is that how you see me? As a shallow, self-centered womanizer?"

She gave his cheek a sisterly pat. "It's what you are. Everybody who knows you knows that. It's the poor fools who don't know you, or who hope to change you, who are in danger of getting hurt by you. That's why Stacey and I always made it a point to warn our friends never to be taken in by those slick lines of yours."

Sterne seized her other hand, imprisoning it in his. Now he held both her hands captive. "You're as smug and arrogant as Zimmer, you nasty little shrew. Maybe I shouldn't have warned you about the bet, after all."

"It wouldn't have mattered either way. I'm not about to succumb to the pseudocharm of a superficial, narcissistic rake."

Sterne arched his brows. "Don't be so sure of that, sweetie."

"I've never been surer of anything in my entire life. Watching the way you've moved in on your conquests and then dropped them cold has been very educational, to say the least. I can hold my own against any ruthless heartbreaker. Now let me go, Sterne."

"So you can go back to your charming prince?"

"King." She smiled thinly. "His name is Daniel King. And yes, I want to go back to him."

"Don't you trust Dr. Wonderful alone in a crowd? Afraid he'll find himself one of the available cuties while you're not there to keep him on his leash?"

Brynn sighed with exasperation. Sterne realized she was beginning to look . . . bored. *Bored?* She was regarding him with the same indifferent irritation with which she might view a squashed mosquito.

Sterne was more than a little irritated himself. The emotions he elicited in women ran the gamut from A to Z, but boredom had never been included in the list. Furthermore, he realized that her sexual awareness of him was nil. It had never bothered him, had never even occurred to him, but now he decided that he didn't like it at all.

She looked at him the same way she looked at his brothers, Spence and Lucas, the same way she looked at her own brother, Brian. No, he decided, he didn't like it at all.

"Don't attribute your own woman-chasing compulsion to Daniel," she said. "*He* has standards and principles." Her tone made it abundantly clear that Sterne Lipton had none of the above and that she'd had enough of their conversation, and of Sterne Lipton himself.

Sterne was irked. He was used to calling the shots. After all, he was the rich bachelor son of the President of the United States. Eminently available, sought-after, and desired, Sterne knew he was appealing to women. They'd been telling him so for years! He was six-one, well-built and muscular, with a shock of light brown hair and deep-set dark blue eyes. Over the years, he'd heard himself described as handsome, attractive, good-looking, and even "yummy!"

The teenaged Brynn and Stacey had collapsed into laughter over that one, Sterne remembered, grimacing. "*Yummy!*" they'd squealed. Then Brynn had poured the remains of her chocolate milkshake over his head. He'd sat stunned with shock, unable to believe that she'd actually had the nerve to do it. But she had and she did. "*Now* you're yummy," she'd said, the sassy little she-devil!

So she didn't consider him dangerous? he mused. She didn't see herself at risk with the man *People* magazine had dubbed the most eligible, elusive, and persuasive bachelor in the country? What if? . . . Sterne gazed down into her green eyes, which were beginning to flash with anger.

What if Little Miss Cassidy were to find herself susceptible to the man she scorned the most? An interesting proposition, he thought, and felt an unaccustomed spark of anticipation. He even had an added incentive to make it happen—the bet with Chambers and Zimmer. The fifteen hundred would be useful in purchasing sheepskin seatcovers for his brand-new lemon-yellow Maserati Bi-Turbo sports car. He was going to have them installed anyway, but there would be an extra kick in knowing they'd been financed by those two blond bozos.

He had originally planned to forget about the bet

after warning Brynn about Zimmer, but the sharp-tongued little termagant had challenged him, hadn't she? And he wasn't a man to let a sexual challenge go unanswered. Sterne was suddenly aware that for the first time in a long, long while, he was no longer bored.

"You're a bully and a creep, Sterne Lipton," Brynn interrupted his reverie, her tone sharp and scolding. "Now let me go!"

"Sorry, baby. Not this time." Impulsively, Sterne scooped Brynn into his arms, then slung her over his shoulder in a fireman's carry. "Your sweet prince will have to find himself other amusement tonight. You're coming with me."

Two

In concession to his position as the president's son, and to monitor any possible threats to his security, Sterne Lipton's Maserati Bi-Turbo sports car was one of the two cars parked directly in front of the Kayes' house. The other was a solid black Mercury sedan belonging to the two Secret Service agents assigned to protect him. As Brynn struggled and howled from her upside-down position over Sterne's shoulder, she caught a glimpse of the dark-suited agents dutifully following them.

"Tell this big gorilla to put me down!" Brynn began to pound on Sterne's back with her fists. "I'm assaulting him!" she announced to the agents. "Aren't you going to come to his aid and get me away from him?"

Neither agent reacted. Obviously, watching Sterne Lipton carry off a woman was commonplace to them. She readdressed her complaints to Sterne. "Bradford Sterne Lipton, Junior, if you don't put me down this minute, I'll—"

"If you don't stop pummeling my kidneys, I'm going to swat your behind!" Sterne interrupted with a growl.

"Just try it!" she dared him, continuing to pummel.

He did. Brynn yelped in furious indignation. Then she was unceremoniously dumped into the bucket seat of Sterne's Maserati.

"Like my new car?" he asked pleasantly as he started the engine.

Brynn, struggling with the seat belt which he'd twisted to impede her escape, didn't bother to answer.

"I particularly like the low-slung seats," he continued chattily as he steered the car along the long, tree-lined driveway. Brynn's attempt to escape had failed. She was stuck with him now. "They're so low-slung that a woman can't get out unless I help her."

Brynn folded her arms across her chest and flashed him a smoldering glance. "Yes, that would appeal to you, wouldn't it? You probably get a chance to peek at their underwear. Big thrill!"

"At times." He smiled wolfishly. "You wouldn't believe what some women wear—or don't wear—under their clothes. What's under yours?"

"Doesn't it ever get boring being a perennial prurient adolescent?"

"Never," Sterne lied.

"Well, I find it boring to be around one. Take me back to the party right now, Sterne."

"I can guarantee that you won't be bored where I'm taking you."

She sighed. "And where is that?"

"To my apartment."

Her eyes widened. "I'm not setting foot in that triple-X-rated den of iniquity you call your apartment!"

He laughed. "That's right, you've never been there, have you? After my stepmother and Stacey's one brief visit, my apartment was declared off-limits to the Lipton clan and their associates."

"No wonder! Stacey told me all about the blonde in the bathtub and the—"

"Stacey and Caroline should've knocked before entering," Sterne cut in. His rakish grin was totally unrepentant. "Don't worry, Brynnie, you won't find anyone waiting for me in my bathtub. That happened back in my wild salad days."

"You've never outgrown your wild salad days," Brynn grumbled. She stared at Sterne for a moment and then the light dawned. Her eyes narrowed and she sat up straight in the black leather bucket seat. "You're involved in this stupid bet, aren't you?" she asked accusingly.

He cleared his throat. "What do you mean?"

"Exactly what I said. When Kyle Zimmer bet Chad Chambers he could get me into bed, you made a wager on it too. And by the way you spirited me away from Zimmer, I can guess that you bet he wouldn't get me into the sack. I'm grateful for that small consideration, at least." She paused. "But you didn't have to kidnap me to assure that you'll win the bet, Sterne. I'm not going to sleep with Kyle Zimmer."

"Indeed you're not," Sterne agreed.

"So drive me back to the party and—"

"No."

"No?" she echoed incredulously. "Sterne, Daniel is there. And he's undoubtedly wondering where I am. He doesn't know anyone at the party and—"

"So?" Sterne shrugged indifferently as he shifted gears. "He'll meet someone."

"I don't *want* him to meet anyone. Not another woman, that is," she amended. "Sterne, do you have any idea how hard it is for a woman to find a nice, normal, potentially marriageable man like Daniel King in the city of Washington? Women outnumber men five—or is it six?—to one here. And the pool of unmarried men is narrowed even further when you take into consideration that some are gay, some are hopeless jerks, some are egocentric womanizers like you, some are—"

"Ever since that survey was published about women's chances for marriage declining statistically each year after the age of twenty-five, every single woman I know is suddenly hot to get married. Don't tell me you've caught the fever, too, Brynnie."

"I'm not being influenced by any survey, Sterne. I simply feel ready for marriage. I feel it's finally the right time for me. I'm twenty-seven years old. I'm tired of dating. I love my job on the House Human Resources Committee and I have good friends, but I want, I *need* something more. I want to share my life with someone I love, someone who loves me. I want to have a family and—"

"I'm sorry I asked," Sterne interrupted. "You sound like you're quoting one of those new greeting cards. 'Feelings cards,' I believe they're called. You know, the kind with the calligraphy and the non-rhyming, wistful messages, and the emotive pastel sketches of couples walking hand-in-hand along the beach."

Brynn felt her face suffuse with color. "I should've known *you* would never understand about feelings and needs. You subscribe to the narcissists' creed. How does it go? 'I am not here to worry about your needs and I don't expect you to worry about mine,' and so on and so on, as you superficially glide through life looking out for Number One."

Sterne knew exactly what she was referring to—the poster he'd kept in his old room at the Lipton house. *I am not here to worry about your needs and I don't expect you to worry about mine.* And so on and so on. He liked the verse so much he'd hung the poster in his apartment, the one she'd never been inside. "There's nothing narcissistic about it," he retorted. "It's a philosophy of honesty and independence."

"Set it to music and you have the anthem of the emotionally shallow."

"My opinion about serious involvement simply differs from yours," he said through clenched teeth. "I feel that a commitment to one person . . . severely limits one's options."

"You want physical intimacy without the risk of emotional involvement, and you want pleasure without emotional investment in another person. You're self-involved, cynical, and shallow."

"Look, if you're trying to annoy me, you're beginning to succeed." He braked the car to a stop at the traffic light of a large intersection. He was seldom roused to anger—usually he shrugged off insults with his characteristic indifference—but he had to admit that Brynn's bald pronouncements were starting to annoy him.

"Only *beginning* to succeed?" she said mockingly. "How much further do I have to go to fully succeed?" She abruptly leaned across the seat and yanked the keys from the ignition. The car's engine spluttered and died. "This far? Have I succeeded? Are you annoyed yet, Sterne?"

Momentarily speechless with shock, Sterne stared from the keyless ignition to his gold key ring held tightly in Brynn's palm. The traffic light turned from red to green. The lemon-yellow Maserati didn't move.

"Give me my keys!" he managed to say in a raspy voice. No one, but no one, had ever violated any of his treasured cars in any way.

"No," Brynn replied succinctly.

The drivers behind them started to blow their horns. A few cars pulled around them. "Dammit, Brynn, give me my keys!" Sterne felt a sudden wave of fury crash over him and its intensity left him reeling. He was thoroughly unaccustomed to strong feelings of any kind. He made a grab for the keys. Brynn artfully swept them out of his reach.

"I want to drive," she said. It was the only way she could think of to avoid being taken to his odious apartment.

"What?" Sterne was so enraged he could barely squeak out that one syllable. He lunged for the keys again and once more failed to retrieve them. He knew he could easily overpower Brynn, but despite his irritation with her, he was reluctant to manhandle her. The blaring car horns echoed in his head. Brynn merely sat smiling and clutching the keys.

It was that maddening little smile of hers that was almost his undoing. He cursed. Her smile widened. He threatened. She laughed. The light changed from green to yellow and back to red, and they continued to sit in the motionless car.

There was a knock on the window. One of the Secret Service agents, who'd been following in the car behind them, stood outside. Sterne groaned and reluctantly rolled down his window. "Is there something wrong with the car, Sterne?" the agent asked solicitously.

"No," Sterne growled.

"No?" The agent looked baffled.

"The car's fine. It just won't run without the keys," Brynn said cheerfully. "And I have the keys." She held them up, jangling them, deliberately tantalizing Sterne. He knew he was being set up, but he couldn't help himself. He snatched wildly for the keys. And missed. He heard a muffled guffaw from the Secret Service agent and his humiliation was complete.

"Are you going to let me drive?" Brynn asked.

"Let *you* drive my brand new car?" Sterne was aghast. "I've seen that banged-up Chevy Nova wreck of yours. You'll never get behind the wheel of my car, lady."

"Then we'll sit here all night, because I'm not giving up the keys unless I can drive." She was not going to Sterne Lipton's apartment!

Sterne was acutely conscious of the Secret Service agent, listening to every word. He was probably mentally cheering Brynn on, he thought crossly. He knew the agents assigned to him didn't approve of him or his freewheeling lifestyle. Conservative, married agents had been assigned to him, for Pete's sake! His request for single, party-going types had been tersely refused.

"I'll never let you drive!" he said in a thundering voice. "You're not going to smash up my new car!"

"I'm a good driver. Although I do have a little trouble with depth perception," Brynn admitted calmly. "But that isn't why my car is dented. That happened in the parking lot at the mall. A van was backing up and—"

"I don't care what happened!" Sterne interrupted desperately. "Just give me my keys so we can get out of here!"

The light had changed to green once more. The honking resumed as the other cars began to pull around them. "Sterne, maybe you'd better let her drive," the agent suggested. He was smirking.

Sterne glanced at the man. "When I want your advice, I'll ask for it!" he snapped. He turned back to Brynn. "Listen to me, you obstreperous, obnoxious little monster. If you don't hand over those keys this minute, I'll—I'll—"

"You'll what?" Brynn asked interestedly.

Sterne's hands were shaking. His whole body was flushed with rage. He couldn't remember the last time he'd felt so angry, so . . . anything. His detachment was a self-protective shield against emotion, for he'd learned long ago that emotional detachment guaranteed freedom from pain. Detachment, control. He felt both slipping.

"All right, dammit, you can drive!" He knew he really had no choice, and it galled him. The only person in the world as stubborn as Brynn Cassidy was his sister Stacey, and Stacey's stubbornness was family legend. Brynn was perfectly capable of keeping them both stuck here in the middle of Georgia Avenue all night unless he let her drive. This was her revenge for taking her away from the party against her will, he guessed. He'd never dreamed she would resort to such measures, for nobody stood up to the son of a famous, powerful man. Sterne Lipton customarily did whatever he wanted without fear of reprisal. He would let Brynn drive now and exact *his* revenge on her later.

Sterne climbed out of the low-slung seat and slammed the door so hard the whole car rattled. He and the agent started to walk behind the car to the passenger side when, quick as a flash, Brynn jumped across the console into the driver's seat.

Did she dare? Brynn wondered. Her heart was pounding. She turned the key in the ignition and engaged the clutch. The engine roared to life. Yes, she decided, she did dare. The Secret Servicemen's car was right behind them. It wasn't as if she were abandoning Sterne to the public at large. The light turned green and Brynn took a deep breath, shifted gears, and the Maserati roared off into the night.

Sterne's shouts of rage echoed in her ears, and she glanced into the rearview mirror to see him shaking his fists and bellowing. She giggled. He reminded her a little of Rumpelstiltskin when the princess had guessed his name. Both compulsive game-players, neither Sterne nor Rumpelstiltskin liked being bested in their games, she thought, grinning.

Brynn drove directly back to the Kayes' party, which was still going strong. She searched the gardens and the entire downstairs of the house, but there was no sign of Daniel King.

Laura Chambers, the Senator's willowy blond daughter and Chad's sister, approached her with an air of urgency. "Come upstairs, Brynn, I have to talk to you," she said.

Brynn followed Laura upstairs to an empty bedroom. Laura closed the door and nervously twisted her hands. "Brynn, this isn't easy for me to say."

"What is it, Laura?" Brynn asked quietly.

"This is so embarrassing. And I'm terribly ashamed of my brother, but . . . Brynn, Chad and Kyle Zimmer made a bet that—that—" Laura broke off, her face scarlet.

Brynn took pity on her. "I know about the bet, Laura. Sterne told me."

Laura's jaw dropped. "*Sterne* told you?"

Brynn nodded. "But I appreciate the warning, anyway. Don't worry, Kyle Zimmer isn't going to win that bet. Sterne is."

Laura gasped. "You—You're going to let Sterne . . ." Her voice trailed off and she stared at Brynn in horrified amazement. "Oh, Brynn, you're making a big, big mistake. I know you must be upset that your date went off with Nicolette Sarsen, but that's no reason to—"

"*My date*—Do you mean Daniel King? He went off with Nicolette *who?*"

"Daniel King, the doctor you introduced me to earlier," Laura confirmed gloomily. "He couldn't find you and asked me if I'd seen you. Nicolette Sarsen happened to be standing with me. She offered to help him look for you. The next thing I knew they were dancing. They left together shortly afterward."

"Oh!" Brynn sank down onto the bed. "I didn't think that Daniel was the type to—to—"

"Brynn, have you ever seen Nicolette Sarsen?" Laura asked.

Brynn shook her head.

"She's Senator Capshaw's twenty-one-year-old niece. She graduated last month from a women's college in the South and just started working in her uncle's office. How can I describe her? She's gorgeous. She's adorable. She has huge brown eyes and a perfectly captivating smile and fairly drips with sweet Southern charm. Even her voice is cute."

"But Daniel is almost thirty," Brynn said. "He's mature and stable and . . ."

"Ready to settle down?" Laura guessed. "Too bad he met Nicolette. She looks like a model for the cover of *Bride's Magazine*. And she's not here in D.C. to pursue a career, Brynn. Her uncle told my father that the family hopes Nicolette will be married by Christmas."

Brynn gulped. "Christmas?"

"She's a sweet girl. An old-fashioned girl. She refused to date my brother because she heard he had a, quote, bad reputation, end quote."

"And Daniel seemed to like her?"

"He was in a daze when he left with her. Nicolette has that kind of effect on men. I've been watching it happen ever since she arrived on the Hill. She's so damned *appealing*! I'm sorry, Brynn." Laura lit a cigarette and sat down beside her on the bed. "But that's no reason to and sleep with Sterne Lipton," she added firmly.

"Sleep with Sterne?" echoed Brynn incredulously. "Of course I wouldn't! He's like a brother to me. An infuriating, licentious one, but a brother, nonetheless."

Laura looked confused. "But you said that you were going to let Sterne win the bet."

It took a second or two to register, and then the impact of Laura's statement hit with full force. "*Sterne bet Kyle Zimmer and Chad that he could get me into bed?*"

"Within two weeks," Laura said. "There's fifteen hundred dollars riding on it. I'm thoroughly disgusted with both Chad and Kyle. How could they involve themselves in something so—so—"

"Sleazy? Shallow?" Brynn suggested tightly. "Exactly Sterne's type of venture. I should've known he was one of the participants!"

"What are you going to do?" Laura asked curiously. "Tell his folks? They'd be properly appalled. They like you better than they like Sterne, anyway."

"No, I'm not going to bother President and Mrs. Lipton with it," Brynn said slowly. Laura was right. Sterne's parents would be appalled, but not surprised. Neither approved of Sterne's sybaritic lifestyle. They viewed it—and him—as a political liability. For as long as Brynn had known the Liptons, Sterne had been at odds with his father's traditional, conservative image.

"Brynn, there's another reason why I told you about that awful bet. About Kyle Zimmer . . ."

"Ugh!" Brynn made a face. "What about him?"

"I'm going to marry him."

It was Brynn's turn to stare, her mouth agape.

"Oh, he doesn't know it yet." Laura managed a slight laugh. "But it's going to happen. If I start coming on to him and make it clear that I'm seriously interested in him, what choice does he have? Kyle's very ambitious. He won't turn down his boss's daughter."

Brynn was aghast. "Laura, why? You don't have to settle for a—a Kyle Zimmer!"

"I'll be thirty next month, Brynn. You have a few more years before you hit it, but believe me, it's hitting me hard. I'm tired of dating games, and relationships that don't work out. I'm tired of trying to compete with a fresh crop of sweet young Nicolette Sarsen types every year. I want to get married and have children, and Kyle Zimmer looks like my best hope right now. So, if you don't mind leaving the field clear for me . . . You see, I know he's attracted to you. That's how the whole stupid bet came about in the first place."

Brynn stared at Laura and felt totally depressed. Laura was pretty and bright and politically well-connected. Surely she needn't corner her father's media consultant into marriage! But she understood the other woman's desire for commitment, for a family. Wasn't that the basis of Daniel King's appeal for herself? Hadn't she been trying to explain her own similar feelings to Sterne tonight? And he'd accused her of sounding like a "feelings" card!

Now Daniel had been captivated by irresistibly adorable Nicolette Sarsen and Sterne . . . Brynn was overcome by a sudden surge of indignant rage. Sterne Lipton, her best friend's brother, was betting on her sexual capitulation—to him!

"After all," Laura continued, her voice rising with determination, "Stacey Lipton married her father's chief administrative aide and that's turned out fine."

"Laura, the situation is totally different. Justin Marks had been crazy about Stacey for years. And he certainly wasn't the type who made bets on taking women to bed! Their marriage is working out because they love each other." Brynn thought of her closest friend's marriage and smiled. Stacey and Justin Marks were a shining example of marriage and commitment at its best, of what she wanted for herself. Brynn knew she couldn't settle for anything less. She wished that Laura felt the same.

"So what are you going to do about Sterne and his bet?" Laura asked, turning the conversation away from herself and her plans for the future and back to Brynn and the present dilemma.

"I don't know." Brynn frowned. "I haven't come up with anything terrible enough yet."

"I have an idea!" Laura exclaimed. "Make Sterne fall for you, and then drop him and laugh in his face! Oh, that would be a fitting revenge! Half of Washington would celebrate if Sterne Lipton was brought to his knees by a woman!"

"Sterne, fall for me?" Brynn laughed. "That's preposterous, Laura."

"He made that bet, didn't he? He must feel some attraction to you."

"Laura, I'm like a kid sister to Sterne. One that he's not particularly crazy about, at that."

"But you *aren't* his kid sister. And he *did* make that bet."

"Laura, I don't want anything to do with Sterne Lipton. In the immortal words of sweet little Nicolette, 'he has a bad reputation.' End quote."

Laura laughed. "You know, I have a feeling that Sterne Lipton might've met his match in you, Brynn. I'll even make a bet on it. Why should the guys be the only ones to make tasteless bets?"

"Count me out, Laura."

"I'll bet you a set of Pratesi sheets that you can bring Sterne Lipton to heel, Brynn."

"Sterne Lipton *is* a heel, Laura, and I don't want any part of any bet. Anyway, I can't afford Pratesi sheets."

"Then you'd better tame Sterne Lipton, hadn't you? That way I'll be buying the Pratesis. King, queen, or double? Any particular color or design?"

"Laura!" Brynn's attempt to reprimand her was foiled by her own sense of humor. The notion of Brynn Cassidy and Sterne Lipton attempting to outmaneuver each other to win respective bets with the Chambers siblings carried ridiculousness to new heights.

"Be firm, kind, and, above all, consistent," Laura advised. "That's what the instructor told me when I enrolled my Lhasa Apso in obedience school."

"That's the way to tame a dog. Sterne's a rat."

Laura grinned. "Then be inconsistent. Keep him off balance. Oh, I can't wait, Brynn! Seeing Sterne Lipton out of his head over a woman will be—"

"I don't want Sterne out of his head over me, Laura."

"He enabled adorable Nicolette to swipe Daniel King from you," Laura reminded her. "At this very moment, he's probably plotting his next move in his campaign to get you to bed. He's planning to use you to win a bet, Brynn! This time he's gone too far—you should be outraged. *I'm* outraged on your behalf!" She strode purposefully to the door. "Do it, Brynn. Teach Sterne Lipton how it feels to fall in love! And *lose*!"

Three

The one place she didn't dare to go was her apartment, Brynn decided as she drove from the Kayes' suburban home into the city. Sterne probably had the place surrounded. She knew that as far as he was concerned, she'd committed the one unspeakable sin in his eyes—she'd driven his car.

She was well aware of Sterne's passion for cars. He treated them with more respect and consideration than he did the multitudinous women who passed in and out of his life. But his basic philosophy toward both cars and women was essentially the same: a trade-in was necessary whenever the novelty began to wear off.

Brynn pressed her foot onto the accelerator and the little car picked up speed. Sterne Lipton was exactly like his flashy cars, she thought, seething. Sleek and attractive and devoid of human feeling. He'd known her since she was a little girl! How could he bet on taking her to bed? The more she thought about it, the angrier she became.

She flexed her fingers on the wheel, thinking of Laura

Chambers urging her to teach Sterne Lipton a lesson in love. What an impossibility! It would be as futile as trying to teach virtue to the devil. Sterne Lipton didn't know what love was and doubtless was uninterested in finding out.

However . . . Her lips curved slowly into a smile. He did have one weak spot, and she was driving it. Brynn flicked on the radio to a soul station and the powerful voice of Aretha Franklin blared through the speakers. "Who's Zoomin' Who?" the singer asked challengingly. Brynn arched her eyebrows. Indeed.

He'd hardly slept a wink all night. Bleary-eyed, Sterne glanced at the clock as he paced through his apartment. Seven A.M. He rarely spent a sleepless night. When he went to bed, he was usually sufficiently exhausted from an evening's partying and sex that he fell asleep instantly, his mind too numbed for the kind of ruminating that produced tossing and turning in the lonely hours of the night.

But last night he'd been so damned infuriated with Brynn for suckering him out of his car that he'd been unable to indulge in his customary pleasures. He'd called three different women, each of whom had offered to come to him immediately, and then he'd called them all back because the thought of having to perform sexually for anyone was totally unappealing. He felt—Damn, *that* was the problem!

He was *feeling*, and he didn't like it. Normally, he could sexually dazzle a woman and satisfy himself physically, all the while operating on automatic pilot. His emotions were never engaged. When his brother Spence, two years younger and heavily into things like feelings and experiencing and being one with the universe, had called him emotionally anesthetized, Sterne had wholeheartedly agreed.

He liked it that way. It was so much easier, so much less messy. He felt superior to those poor fools who were at the mercy of their emotions, always up or down, hurting, crying, feeling pain . . .

Sterne fixed a cup of instant coffee and cursed Brynn Cassidy. It was all her fault, dammit! She'd made him angrier than he had any right to be, and the anger was burning him, melting away his protective indifference, his comfortable apathy.

He was furious and he was frustrated. He wanted his car and he couldn't have it. He didn't handle frustration well, Sterne admitted to himself with a flash of insight. Another anomaly. He wasn't given to flashes of insight. His defenses slammed shut. He didn't care for flashes of insight. They inevitably led to pain.

The telephone rang three hours later. "Yeah?" Sterne barked into the receiver, looking forward to the chance to take out his frustrations on whoever the hapless caller might be.

"Do you want your car back?" Brynn asked coolly.

"You!" Sterne's pulse began to pound. He could actually hear his heart thundering in his chest. "Where the hell have you been, you—you—"

"Your car is in a parking lot at National Airport," Brynn interrupted his tirade in the same cool tones. And then she hung up.

The click seemed to resound in his ears. "Wait a minute," he bellowed. "Which parking lot? Do you know how many there are at National?"

There was only a dial tone. His hand shaking with rage, Sterne dialed Brynn's number. He knew it by heart now, after having dialed it all night. It was the only phone number he'd ever memorized besides his own and the National Weather Service's.

There was no answer at Brynn's. She either wasn't there or was ignoring the persistent ringing. After letting it ring one hundred and twelve times, Sterne concluded that she wasn't home. *No one* could listen to a phone ring one hundred and twelve times without picking it up.

• • •

A loud, persistent buzzing intruded on Brynn's deep, dreamless sleep. At first she moaned softly and turned over, fighting the forces that were rousing her to wakefulness. It was no use, though. Her eyes opened slowly and she gazed drowsily around the room.

The floor-to-ceiling shelves on the wall opposite her bed were filled to overflowing with dogs. Stuffed dogs and porcelain dogs, carved wooden dogs and china dogs of very size and breed. She'd been collecting toy dogs since she'd been a child, and someday she hoped to realize her dream and have a real one.

The buzzing that had awakened her was her door-bell, and Brynn ran a hand through her tousled hair on her way to answer it. She was wearing loosely cut white cotton shorts and an oversized white-and-tur-quoise-striped cotton shirt, both wrinkled from having been slept in. She couldn't remember the last time she'd taken an afternoon nap—kindergarten, perhaps? —but she'd been so exhausted from her near-sleepless night that she'd fallen asleep the moment she'd laid down on her bed almost four hours earlier.

Brynn flung open the door. Sterne Lipton, dressed in black jeans and an unbuttoned and untucked black shirt, was lounging against the door jamb, his thumb on the bell. Brynn blinked. He was soaking wet.

Her brain was still cloudy with sleep. "Is it raining?" she asked.

"Pouring," Sterne replied grimly. "I spent the past three and a half hours in it as I searched every damn parking lot at National Airport for my car."

Brynn's brain cleared a little. "Did you find it?"

"Yeah." He took the tails of his shirt and wrung them out. Water splashed onto the floor. He was thoroughly soaked. "I found it. Tucked between two vans, making it damned near impossible to spot, despite its color. And it was in the last parking lot I tried, naturally! Thanks a million for locking the keys inside, Brynn. I had to break a window to get in. I'll send you the bill. Along with the fifteen-dollar parking fee."

"I won't pay either one," she retorted. "At least you got your car back. All's well that ends well, hmm?"

He pushed past her into the apartment. "Oh, it's not over yet, sweetie. Not by a long shot." He stepped out of his shoes, which sloshed with the water they'd absorbed. He wasn't wearing socks, of course. Sterne didn't believe in socks, except in the dead of winter. He shrugged out of his shirt, dropping it onto the floor. Next, he purposefully unfastened the heavy silver buckle on his thick, black leather belt.

Brynn was staring at him. "What are you doing, Sterne?"

The fly of his jeans was fastened with heavy metal buttons. He proceeded to undo them, one by one. "What does it look like I'm doing, Brynn?"

"It looks like you're undressing."

"Bingo. The lady got it in one."

His jeans hit the floor. He stepped out of them, clad only in a pair of black bikini underpants. Brynn drew in a sharp breath. "I suppose I should be thankful that at least you're wearing underwear. Remember when you told the reporter from *Cosmo* that you seldom do?"

"Because it's too constricting and confining." He grinned in spite of himself. "Yeah, I remember. And I remember how everything hit the fan when she printed it on page one. Poor Roland Hobart was not pleased!"

"Poor" Roland Hobart was President Lipton's press secretary, the unfortunate soul who had to deal with the media's response to the various exploits of the Lipton offspring. Brynn knew it was not an enviable position.

"Do you mind telling me why you've stripped and left your soaking wet clothes on my rug?" she asked calmly.

"What? No shocked gasp? Not even a maidenly blush? I'm disappointed in your reaction, Brynn."

"I've been dealing with Liptons for the past fifteen years, Bradford Sterne Lipton, Junior. I'm way past shocked gasps and maidenly blushes when it comes to all of you. Anyway . . ." She tossed her head and her bright hair fell forward in a thick curtain. "It looks like you're wearing a bathing suit and I've seen you in a bathing suit before. You always did go in for the skimpy ones. Showing off your marvelous physique to your hordes of female admirers, I guess?"

"So you admit I have a marvelous physique."

Her gaze flicked over him. His shoulders were broad and muscular, his chest hard and covered with dark, curling hair which tapered into his low-slung briefs. His stomach was corded and flat, his navel deeply indented. His hips were narrow, and the long, lean, and muscled legs were covered with a fine layer of lighter, curling hair.

She shrugged. "You're not bad. You look athletic, like you work out a lot. And watch your weight."

"I don't have to watch my weight!" Sterne said, annoyed. "I eat whatever I want and—"

"Work it off in bed with a willing partner," she finished for him. "I know, I know, I've heard that particular bit before. Except you usually accompany it with a carefully executed lascivious wink."

"Exactly *what* is a carefully executed lascivious wink?" he demanded.

She showed him. Sterne laughed. He hadn't intended to. He was furious with her. She'd caused him to spend hours in the pouring rain searching for his car, she'd caused him a miserable sleepless night. And now she was making fun of him. But he laughed at her imitation of him carefully executing a lascivious wink, anyway.

Recovering himself, he tried to get his anger back on track. "Do you have any idea how much I hated you this afternoon as I tramped through miles of parking lot in a monsoon looking for the car you stole from me?"

She flopped down on the sofa. "You deserved it and worse, Sterne Lipton."

"The hell I did, Brynnie." He flopped down beside her. "Where were you last night, anyway? I tried calling all night. There was no way you could've been here and gotten any sleep with me calling every fifteen minutes and letting the phone ring for ten."

He sat up straight, a thought suddenly dawning. "You went back to the party, didn't you? And picked up your date! That's where you were all last night—with him!" His anger, simmering slightly beneath the surface, came to a roaring boil.

She'd had the nerve to drive another man in *his* car! He pictured the two of them cruising the beltway, laughing, talking, playing the stereo cassette deck, and fury crashed over him. Brynn and another man—in his car!

"You little witch!" He grabbed her shoulders and jerked her toward him. As he stared into her wide green eyes another image of her was superimposed over her startled expression. He saw her again as she'd opened the door to him a few minutes earlier. He'd been too consumed with his anger and his wet clothes to notice her drowsy stare, her cheeks flushed from sleep, her attractively tousled hair. She'd looked soft and cuddly—and sexy as hell! He imagined she'd look like that waking from sleep after a long, satisfying session of lovemaking.

No, he hadn't consciously noticed her then, but his brain seemed to have photographed the image and insisted upon playing it back for him, over and over. *She'd looked that way last night, in her lover's bed!* His stomach began to churn. The blood thundered through his veins and echoed in his head. He was jealous! He recognized the emotion from the long-ago days when he'd permitted himself to feel. Heaven help him, he was jealous!

His first instinct was to run—but his clothes lay in a sodden heap on the floor. Then he became shatteringly aware of her nearness. His fingers tightened on her shoulders. Suddenly, he was having trouble breathing. He inhaled shakily and his nostrils filled with the scent of her, a totally unerotic combination of soap and shampoo. It aroused him more intensely than the expensive, exotic fragrances used by other women he had known.

Her eyes were huge and green, her skin soft and smooth. He stared at the sweet, full curves of her parted lips, and he imagined sliding his tongue into the moist warmth of her mouth. Desire crashed through him with a dizzying intensity. He wanted to taste her, to feel her trembling beneath him, to hear her moan his name as he sheathed himself in her soft, feminine heat.

His body hardened; his anticipation grew. He wanted her, he realized with thunderstruck wonder. He wanted her badly. "Oh, baby," he groaned as a surge of desire shot through him.

"Forget it, Sterne!" Brynn braced her hands on his chest and gave him a forceful push. Her resistance was so unexpected that she knocked him off balance and he fell backward against the sofa cushions.

She stood up, glowering at him. "I know all about the bet, Sterne. Your part included. Laura Chambers told me everything last night."

"The bet?" he repeated slowly. His body was throbbing, his breathing shallow. When was the last time he'd been so quickly and so forcefully aroused? He'd barely touched her; he'd certainly not been holding her in a sexual way. Yet his senses had been full of the scent and the feel of her, and his desire had been kindled like a match against flint.

It *had* been years since that had happened, Sterne realized nervously. He was the first to admit that his sexual responses had become jaded over the years. He needed heightened thrills to arouse him, to satisfy him. Yet merely being near Brynn had aroused him to the point of aching. First had come anger, then jealousy, and now pure and undiluted throbbing desire. He felt panic grow within him. Was he on the edge of losing his grip?

"Don't try to pretend you don't know what I'm talking about," Brynn said severely. "You bet Kyle Zimmer one thousand dollars that you'd have me in bed within two weeks."

"It wasn't like you think," Sterne mumbled. "I never intended to go through with it."

"Oh, *ha!* Here you sit in your underwear after making a grab for me, and I'm supposed to believe that you don't intend to try to collect? Give me an unusually large break, Sterne."

The worst part of it, he thought glumly, was that he hadn't been thinking of the bet at all when that fierce shaft of desire had surged through him. He'd wanted her, and there had been no ulterior motive urging him on. Thank heaven *she* didn't know that! He was thoroughly disconcerted.

Brynn was thoroughly infuriated. She stomped over to his pile of clothes and picked up the black shirt and jeans. "I'm going to run these through the dryer and then you're going to put them on and leave!"

Sterne watched her storm from the room. He was glad to see her go. Was it possible, he wondered as anxiety knotted in his chest, that he was having some sort of breakdown? No woman had ever affected him this way before. He stared down at the evidence of his urgent arousal and a chill ran through him.

Brynn hadn't even noticed! She was as sexually unaware of him as he'd been of her—until now. Or had his awareness of her begun last night? He remembered looking at her at the party and seeing her as a stranger would, as an appealing, attractive, desirable young woman. A sexy redhead, Zimmer had said, and Sterne's lifetime perception of Brynn had been irrevocably altered.

What now? he wondered in a frantic mixture of frustration and confusion. He was used to getting what he wanted, either by taking it or having it given to him.

It wasn't going to work that way with Brynn. He knew her well enough to know that she wouldn't give herself to him. He had all the appeal of typhoid fever for her. Just last night she'd lambasted him for being shallow, self-involved, and cynical. And heaven help him if he tried to take her and she didn't want to be taken! Brynn was not one to capitulate meekly. She was more likely to turn homicidal on him.

He heard the telephone ring, heard Brynn walk from the kitchen to the bedroom to answer it. Then he heard her voice, light and sweet, exclaim happily, "Oh, hi, Daniel!"

Sterne stood up and strode toward the bedroom.

Brynn was sitting on the narrow single bed, holding the receiver. Sterne stood in the doorway, legs apart and arms folded in an aggressive stance. He glanced at the menagerie of dogs on the shelves without really seeing them. Daniel, the princely doctor, was on the phone, he thought. The man whom Brynn had decided would be just perfect to settle down and have children with. The man she'd spent last night with!

Brynn glared at Sterne and turned away from him. She did not care to have a witness to this conversation. Particularly as Daniel King was doing nothing but raving about adorable, sweet, beautiful, and irresistible Nicolette Sarsen!

"At first I was upset when Violet Kaye told me she'd seen you leaving the party with Sterne Lipton," Daniel confessed blithely. "But if you hadn't left, I wouldn't have met Nicolette. It was fate, Brynn. Destiny. I know that now. Nicolette and I were meant to meet at that party. And I just called to thank you for inviting me to it."

And to let me know that I won't be hearing from you anymore, Brynn mentally added, *because you've met the girl of your dreams.* Her jaw tightened. She'd liked Daniel King. He was nice and normal and marriageable. Her green eyes flashed. Daniel was everything that cad Sterne Lipton was not! And it was all Sterne's fault that Nicolette Sarsen would be married by Christmas, just like her family had planned. She'd be married to Daniel King.

"Maybe we can get together sometime, Brynn," Daniel continued, sounding boyishly eager. "You and your date, and Nicolette and me." He was in love and fairly bursting with it. He obviously thought that everyone would be enchanted to meet his darling.

Brynn winced. She was not enchanted. "Great. Let's do lunch sometime."

Daniel didn't even catch her sardonic tone. He went off on another tangent, rhapsodizing about Nicolette's charms.

" 'Let's do lunch?' " Sterne repeated when Brynn had hung up. "You sound like a Hollywood agent. Hardly the way a woman speaks to her lover."

"And you'd know all about that, wouldn't you?" Brynn scowled. "Thanks to you, Daniel isn't my lover and he isn't going to be. He's going to be Nicolette Sarsen's husband."

"But you spent the night with him last night."

"I spent the night with two girlfriends of mine, Bernadette Nicotero and Mary Jo Flanagan. I slept on their sofa bed. Well, we really didn't sleep much." Brynn half smiled in reminiscence. Last night had been rather like an old-fashioned slumber party, the three of them talking and watching movies on TV and snacking till close to dawn. "I knew I couldn't come back here since I had your car, so I hid out at their place."

"You were a bad little girl to steal my car," Sterne said silkily, moving toward her. "How are you going to make it up to me?" His big hands encircled her waist. She was soft and small and slender.

And she didn't want him. Brynn removed his hands and glared at him. "Kindly spare me your flirtatious repartee. I'm already feeling nauseated from that conversation with Daniel. You're going to make me acutely ill."

"Daniel's a fool to prefer—what's her name? Nicole?—to you," Sterne said, settling his hands on her hips. His thumbs rested on her abdomen and he began to knead the firm skin through the thin cotton.

"Her name is Nicolette and *you're* a fool if you think

I'm going to let you use me to win a bet with Kyle Zimmer and Chad Chambers." Brynn pushed him away and stalked out of the bedroom.

He followed her into the kitchen. "I'll call Zimmer and tell him the bet's off."

"Fine, you do that." She retrieved his jeans and shirt from the dryer. Both were still damp, but she didn't care. She tossed the clothes at him. "Get dressed and get out of here, Sterne."

"I mean it, Brynn. I'll call off the bet with Zimmer."

"If?" she prompted caustically.

"If what?"

"You tell me. You've never done anything in your life unless there was something in it for you."

"You don't have a very high opinion of me, Brynn," he said reproachfully.

"How true. And it's getting lower by the minute."

They glared at each other. What an egotistical skunk he was! Brynn thought with amazement. He actually believed he could win that bet! *When hell freezes over, Lipton,* she silently promised him.

Sterne stared at the stubborn set of her jaw, at her mouth which was twisted with outrage. She was looking at him as if he were a cockroach, or something lower. She wasn't the sexy, sloe-eyed temptress he thought he'd seen earlier, she was the Brynn he'd known for years. How could he have ever thought, even for a few misguided moments, that he wanted her? She was just little Brynnie, his baby sister's bratty friend. What on earth was he doing here? He glanced around, feeling strangely disoriented.

The doorbell rang, and Brynn left the kitchen without a word. A moment later, Sterne heard Kyle Zimmer's voice at the front door.

"Uh, hi, Brynn."

Brynn stared at Kyle Zimmer and suppressed a sigh. "It never rains," she muttered under her breath. First Sterne Lipton in his underwear, then the phone call from Daniel King extolling Nicolette's charms, now Kyle Zimmer here to try to win the bet with Sterne. "It pours."

Kyle heard her and misunderstood. "It certainly is pouring out there," he said quickly. "I had to park my car half a block away and got soaked dashing from there into the building. Brynn, I brought you these." He thrust a long white florist's box into her arms.

She thrust it back at him. "I don't want flowers from you, Kyle. I just want you to leave."

"But, Brynn . . ."

She sighed. "I know all about the bet, Kyle."

"I know." He had the grace to look ashamed. "Laura told me last night. Brynn, I want you to know that I never intended to become involved in anything so—so—"

"Sleazy and shallow? Disgusting, degrading, and dehumanizing?"

Kyle reddened. "I guess that about sums it up. I'm sorry, Brynn."

"So am I," she agreed dryly.

"Will you accept my apology and my roses and let me try to make amends?" Kyle asked, bestowing his most winning smile on her. "I was attracted to you from the moment I saw you at the party last night and I'd like to get to know you, Brynn. Will you give me that chance, even though I don't deserve it?"

The jerk was covering all the bases, Sterne thought, fuming, as he eavesdropped in the kitchen. The nerve of the guy, coming to Brynn's apartment with roses and humble apologies! Did he actually think he had a chance with her? Well, Sterne Lipton was here to thwart any such plans!

He strode into the living room, determined but utterly confused as to his motives. Was he a big brother protecting little Brynnie from the blond shark who'd bet he could get her into bed? Or was he a jealous male staking his claim on the beautiful, desirable woman he'd already designated as his property?

Whatever his motivation, Sterne's appearance in his bikini underwear brought an immediate response. "Ohh!" Brynn groaned.

"I see you already have company," Kyle said, tight-lipped. "Do I owe you a thousand dollars, Lipton?"

Sterne stood directly behind Brynn and wrapped his arms around her, drawing her back against his hard, muscular frame. He was careful to lock her arms in his iron grip, thus preventing her from elbowing him in the stomach. Which, he suspected, was probably her greatest wish at this moment.

His big hands closed over her wrists, further inca-pacitating her. Brynn had stiffened with tension—and rage. He knew if he were to let her loose, she would probably mangle him. On the other hand, he decided with pure masculine satisfaction, Zimmer's wide-eyed expression made his impromptu appearance worth any such risk.

"The bet's off, Zimmer," he informed the other man loftily. "I told you Brynnie wasn't that kind of girl."

"You can let me go now, Sterne," Brynn said in dul-cet tones. She slipped her bare foot on top of his and ground her heel into his toes to add emphasis to her request.

"But I love holding you, sweetheart." Sterne hissed in pain as she continued to mash his foot with the force of one stomping grapes. In retaliation, he bent his head and nipped the sensitive skin of her neck. Then he began to lick. And suck.

His sensual retaliation was alarmingly, instantly effective. Brynn reacted as if she'd been struck by lightning. She removed her foot from his and drew in her breath in a startled gasp. She was suddenly intensely aware of the size and strength of the man holding her, of the heat of his hard body. She felt his lips and his teeth and his tongue on her neck, and sharp tendrils of sexual excitement uncurled in her abdomen.

Her knees were rubbery. For one crazy moment, she felt an overwhelming urge to close her eyes and lean against Sterne's solid body, to relax completely and let his arms support her while she gave in to the delicious sensations rippling through her.

"Well." Kyle Zimmer cleared his throat. "I can see that I arrived at an inopportune time. . . ." His face was flushed. He glanced from Sterne to Brynn and frowned.

"Any time is inopportune for you around here, Zimmer," Sterne said. "So long, buddy. And take your roses with you."

"Give them to Laura," Brynn suggested, remembering the other woman's plans for Kyle Zimmer. "I'm sure she'll appreciate them."

Kyle Zimmer left without another word, banging the door behind him. For a split second, neither Sterne nor Brynn moved or spoke.

"I guess we showed him." Sterne was the first to break the silence. "That'll teach him not to come courting after he's made a rude, tasteless bet insulting a lady's virtue."

Brynn didn't mean to laugh. Sterne Lipton was outrageous and incorrigible, a rogue beyond redemption. No one knew it better than she. But she laughed, anyway. She usually ended up laughing with Sterne, she realized in surprise. For reasons she would never begin to understand, he appealed to her sense of humor.

"Ah, Brynnie." He nuzzled her neck and sighed. "What in the hell is happening between us? I thought we were safely immune to each other. We *should* be safely immune to each other. I can't have an affair with you. The family wouldn't stand for it. You mean too much to them."

She stirred in his arms, but he didn't release her. "Believe me, Sterne, I have no intention of having an affair with you."

He pulled her back, holding her closer against him, and continued to nibble on her neck. "That's very wise. You'd probably fall in love with me and be badly hurt when it was over."

"Me? Fall in love with you?" She sniffed. "Not a chance, mister."

"No?" He was kissing her ear now, his tongue making slow, sensual forays into the shell-like cavity. His hands dropped hers and moved upward over her ribcage. "You seem like one of those girls who can't separate love from sex. And you're starting to turn on for me, Brynnie."

She was. She gulped. "Let me go, Sterne. The game's over."

"You're turned on and you know it." He laughed softly against her ear, a sexy, husky sound that sent shivers along her spine.

The man was the quintessential rake, she reminded herself, and never pretended to be otherwise. He was the antithesis of everything she wanted in a man, or from a man. And yet . . . she was starting to respond to him physically. His low voice, his experienced caresses, his dark, forbidding sensuality were exerting a powerful force against her own common sense.

His thumbs brushed over her nipples and she tensed. "Don't!" Her voice was hoarse and thick and Sterne chuckled.

"You're turning on, all right, sweetie. Your body is telling me all I need to know."

His fingers made a lazy circle of her nipples, and she felt them tighten into rigid sensitivity. His teeth were toying with her earlobe.

Drawing in a steadying breath, Brynn took advantage of her freed hands to grasp his wrists and pull his hands away from her breasts. "Quit it, Sterne."

"It's not going to work, Brynnie. You're as curious as I am. We're going to have to do it, you know."

Her heart seemed to come to a screeching halt, then resumed its pounding at a frantic rate. "Oh, no, Sterne Lipton. Bet or no bet, I won't go to bed with you!"

"No, we don't have to take it that far," he said. "A kiss ought to do it."

She turned around in his arms to face him. He linked his hands loosely at the small of her back, and she could've broken away from him, had she thought to do so. She didn't. "What do you mean?" she asked, staring at him intently.

Undeniably, he was a handsome man. For years Brynn had loftily told herself that she didn't care for classically handsome men, that they tended to be as shallow and uninteresting as the bland perfection of their features. But staring up into Sterne's deep, dark blue eyes was making her feel weak.

Her gaze flickered over his mouth and she felt even weaker. His lips were well shaped and sensual, his teeth even and white. For the first time in her life she wondered what it would feel like to have that well-shaped sensual mouth crushing hers.

She felt her lips part. It almost hurt to breathe. Damn, why did he have to be so good-looking? So masculinely appealing? Every one of her nerves seemed poised on a shattering edge. Brynn was horrified by her own sensual urgency, and by her uncharacteristic lack of judgment. What was happening to her? Her brain echoed the lament that Sterne had voiced earlier.

"I mean, let's kiss and get it over with," Sterne answered her question with typical laconic flatness. "The longer we let the sexual tension build between us, the harder it'll be not to give in to it, not to make it into something it isn't. So we'll kiss right now and get it out of our systems."

Brynn regarded him with wide-eyed confusion. "But doesn't a kiss lead to"—she swallowed—"to other things?"

His laugh was brief and mirthless. "I was right about you, Brynnie. You *are* one of those self-deluded girls who have love and sex hopelessly entangled. You think that a kiss builds into passion and—boom—the lovers are swept away by the force of their desires. Then, sigh, comes the happily-ever-after ending. Sorry to shatter your illusions, baby, but it doesn't work that way."

Brynn frowned. Her own desire was rapidly cooling in the chill of his unimpassioned declarations. This was Sterne, her head reminded her overheated body. Cynical, dispassionate *Sterne!* The man who made Don Juan look like a leader in sensitivity training. What was she doing in his arms?

"Kissing is an act in itself," he continued. "It can be pleasurable or boring, but it certainly doesn't inevitably lead to intercourse. I've laid, uh, I mean, made love to a number of women without kissing them once."

"Each one of them has my deepest sympathy," Brynn said through gritted teeth. "Let me go, Sterne. Any remote curiosity I might've had about what it would be like to kiss you has been totally obliterated."

"I'll let you go after I've kissed you," he said calmly.

"Why do you want to kiss me? You'll undoubtedly be bored!"

"Yeah, I know." He smiled grimly. "And then I'll be cured of this stupid whatever-it-is that makes me think that I—I—" He broke off abruptly and frowned. "Quit stalling, Brynnie. The sooner it's over, the sooner I'll be out of here."

Brynn stared up at him. His blue eyes were as remote and cold as an arctic ice cap. He didn't want her. He wanted to kiss her, be bored with the kiss, and leave. She was totally perplexed by his demand. If he was making a pass at her, it was the most cleverly disguised one she'd ever encountered.

His fingers captured her chin and tilted it upward. "Open your mouth," he commanded as his lips descended on hers.

Four

Brynn drew back and managed to evade Sterne's mouth.

"Brynn!" he said impatiently. "Let's not drag this out all day!" One big hand clamped around the nape of her neck and firmly held her head in place as he again lowered his mouth to hers.

Brynn watched, feeling strangely detached from the entire proceedings. "It's just that nothing like this has ever happened to me before," she said as his lips touched hers.

"No?" He nipped at her lips as she spoke.

"Nobody's ever wanted to kiss me with the expressed intention of being bored while doing so." She was, she realized to her surprise, nibbling on Sterne's lips as she talked.

"*Hoping* to be bored," he amended. His fingers kneaded the nape of her neck while his other hand caressed her back in long, slow strokes. "I'd better be bored, honey. You don't want me pursuing you."

"You've never pursued a woman in your life," she retorted. Her arms were around his neck and her fingers threaded through his springy, thick hair. Each word she spoke was punctuated by teasing, biting kisses. "If a woman doesn't come to you when you crook your little finger, you shrug and move on to one who will."

He smiled against her mouth. "How well you know me, Brynnie."

"Too well." Her eyes were half closed. Sterne was feathering the curve of her mouth with his lips, his teeth, and his tongue, and she was responding with soft, butterfly kisses of her own, hot little kisses that teased and tantalized but didn't satisfy. "This is insane, Sterne. For both of us."

Her body wasn't listening. It seemed to have a will of its own. She felt herself lean into his hard body, and he moved against her cushioning softness and groaned. "Insane, but unfortunately not boring, Brynnie-Brynn."

His strong, sensitive fingers took possession of her breasts. "Sweet," he whispered, slipping his tongue into her mouth. He withdrew it just as swiftly, luring hers into following. "Sweet, sweet girl."

"I'm not a girl," she managed to protest. Her tongue darted daringly into his mouth, then quickly retreated. She felt the burgeoning pressure of his thighs against hers. "I grew up years ago."

"And somehow I never noticed until now," he murmured against her mouth.

She felt her breasts swell in the palms of his hands and an intense excitement ran over her skin like fire, making her burn with desire. "Oh, Sterne," she whispered, her tone wondering, as if she were saying his name for the first time.

They gazed at each other for a moment. Brynn was shaking; she couldn't stop. Then Sterne bent his head and his mouth closed fiercely over hers. Her lips, sensitized by their earlier love play, parted instantly as she mindlessly yielded to his hot, hard demands.

His hands slid intimately down her body and heated her skin wherever he touched. The blood sang in her ears and a piercing, throbbing ache grew and expanded deep inside her. She twisted restlessly under his exploring hands, straining to get closer, to have more of him. His musky masculine scent intoxicated her.

His tongue thrust into her mouth, filling her, making her moan and arch against him. Her senses swam, and she ran her hands over the hair-roughened skin of his chest and traced his flat nipples with her thumbs. She'd never felt this way before. She'd never experienced this burning, churning need to toss off all restraint, all control, to stop thinking and simply feel.

She'd always considered herself too levelheaded to be swept away by passion. Now, as she clung to Sterne, meeting his kisses and caresses with hungry abandon, Brynn realized that unconsciously she must have been repressing the sexually passionate side of her nature. Her sensuality had lain slumbering under a mantle of levelheaded common sense, only to be awakened and aroused by . . . Sterne Lipton.

She should be apalled. Sterne was a user. He took and didn't give. He was emotionally aloof and unreachable. It was easy for him to hurt others because he felt no pain himself.

But what she was feeling wasn't one-sided. A primal feminine instinct assured her of that. Brynn could feel Sterne trembling as he held her and she sensed a vulnerability in him that equaled her own. The passion flowing between them was mutual, she was sure of that. He was as emotionally attuned to her as she was to him.

He moved his mouth over hers, changing angles to penetrate more fully the moist softness, to drink deeply of the sweetness she so generously offered. Her body felt warm and vibrant and alive.

She pressed closer, opening her mouth wider, encouraging a deeper, even more intimate kiss. Her passion was tempestuous, and he was swept up in the storm. Little Brynnie, he mused dazedly. Who'd have thought it? He wanted her, wanted her with a force and fervor he hadn't experienced in . . . He couldn't remember the last time he'd felt this forceful, fervent need.

Sterne had always been the master of his passion. Now passion threatened to master him. Who would have dreamed that Brynn could evoke such feelings in him, could smash through his carefully constructed defenses with a kiss, a touch?

They'd known each other for so long. They'd slept under the same roof countless times over the years in various Lipton houses—the beach cottage in Rehoboth, the gracious homestead in Omaha, the luxurious three-story brick colonial in Chevy Chase. They'd eaten breakfast together in their robes, whispered good nights in darkened hallways, sipped each other's drinks, and shared a thousand other intimacies, and he'd never felt a shred of desire for her. Sexual awareness had been cloaked by familial familiarity. Yet now . . .

He wanted her. He had to have her. Who'd have guessed it? Little Brynnie . . . Something stirred within him. Something alarming, something ominous. Something totally unfamiliar and, he sensed, totally dangerous. To him. A lifetime's experience in control enabled him to abruptly put the brakes on his escalating passion. Good Lord! *Little Brynnie!* Had he lost his mind?

Abruptly, Sterne pushed her away from him. Brynn's eyes snapped open, and she looked at him dazedly. Her skin was burning, her body melting.

"Stop looking at me that way," he said hoarsely. His heart was thundering so loudly in his ears that he could hardly hear himself speak. He was trembling, he realized in stunned dismay.

"What way?" Brynn asked, breathless and bewildered. Her face was flushed, her lips softly swollen from his kisses, her green eyes dilated and sleepy with passion. Sterne muttered a curse. "You want me!" He made it sound like an accusation.

Heaven help her, Brynn thought. She did want him. She stared up at Sterne and felt her head spin. His eyes were gorgeous, so deep and dark and blue that one could drown in them. And his mouth . . . Oh, his mouth. She closed her eyes and touched her fingers to her lips as desire tore through her.

Sterne watched her. Her every movement tempted, beckoned. He wanted so much to pull her back into his arms that the sheer force of his longing sent him reeling into an unfamiliar, uncharacteristic panic. "Oh, no, not me!" He backed away from her. "Your price is way too high for me, baby."

She opened her eyes and gazed limpidly at him. "Price?" she echoed in confusion.

"Marriage." He continued to back away from her, putting up his hands, as if to ward her off. "You want to get married," he said in the tone of a police officer issuing an arrest warrant. "And I don't."

The warmth began to drain slowly from her eyes. "I don't recall asking you to marry me."

"But you just gave me the go-ahead, sweetie. If I'm willing to meet your terms, I can have you—the bet and my reputation and every other objection you've ever raised about me be damned."

Brynn straightened. The descent from cloud nine to grim reality was a jarring, painful one. "I don't know what you're talking about!" she managed to say, choking on the words.

The way he was staring at her, with a cynical and all-knowing expression on his face, was making her blush. She never should have responded to him, she thought grimly. She certainly hadn't intended to. But something magical, something intangible yet very real, had swept them both headlong into the turbulent seas of passion.

Turbulent seas of passion? Her blush deepened. Since when had she started thinking in mushy metaphors? The levelheaded Brynn was back, her common sense fully restored. And her pride had returned with a vengeance.

"You'll never have me," she told Sterne haughtily.

"All right, you made me . . . respond to you this one time. Believe me, it'll never happen again. You're very experienced and you hit me with every sexual weapon in your arsenal, but I won't be susceptible again."

Sterne laughed derisively. "You almost make me want to take you up on the challenge. You'd like that, wouldn't you, baby?"

"Stop calling me baby! I hate it. I hate you!"

"You wish you did, baby, but you don't," he said with maddening arrogance. "We both know that I can have you anytime I want. All I did was kiss you and you melted in my arms."

She stared at him, aghast. Over the years, she'd watched and listened to Sterne with his women, alternately feeling sorry for or ridiculing those unfortunate females who allowed themselves to be set up for his insults. *And now she was one of them!* Over the years he had called her a monster and a stupid pest and a conniving brat, and she'd always laughed it off. But this . . .

No woman could put up with such insufferable male arrogance, Brynn decided. No woman should have to. Her temper flared to blowtorch intensity, and she drew back her fist and smacked him. This was no ladylike little slap. She walloped him with every ounce of strength she possessed, acting on behalf of every woman in the world who'd ever been insulted by an insensitive macho clod.

Sterne staggered backward. Yellow spots flashed before his eyes and a wave of dizziness swept over him from the sheer force of the pain. There was a ringing in his ears. Gulping for breath, he sank down onto the sofa.

"Get up!" Brynn was tugging at his arm. "Get out of my apartment, you slug!"

Sterne didn't budge. Lord, she'd hit him hard! She was such a little thing. He'd never dreamed she possessed such strength. His head was still spinning from the force of the blow. When a woman struck a man in the movies, it was inevitably the actor's cue to seize his leading lady in a hot clinch, Sterne thought ironically. The movie script didn't take into consideration the incredible pain of a sharp blow to the face. Right now he felt incapable of standing up. A passionate clinch would be pure agony.

"Sterne?" Brynn's white-hot anger had cooled slightly, enabling her to view Sterne more objectively. He hadn't moved from the sofa. "You're looking a little pale," she said. "You're not going to faint, are you?"

He groaned. "If I do, I'll contact a hit man and arrange for my own demise. I don't want to live in a world where I faint after you've clobbered me. I'm humiliated enough as it is. Damn, you belted me, Brynnie! I think you gave me a black eye."

She examined his face dispassionately. "I'm afraid you are going to have a nasty bruise."

He groaned again. "Will you go along with my explanation that I walked into a door?"

She sat down beside him. "Why not add a little dashing machismo to your story? You could say you were attacked by a gang carrying tire irons as you rushed to the aid of the little old lady they were mugging."

Sterne lightly touched his eye and winced. "I don't find anything amusing about this, Brynn."

She nodded her agreement. "Particularly not those intolerable remarks you made to me."

"Ah, Brynnie, I say things like that all the time." He sighed. "You shouldn't have taken it personally."

"Well, I did."

"Yeah, I noticed." He rubbed the side of his face. "Damn, it hurts, Brynn."

"I'll get you an icepack." She left, and returned a few minutes later with a filled round blue icebag. Sterne was lying on the sofa. He took the icebag and laid it over his eye. "I need something for the pain. How about a double shot of whiskey?"

"I don't have any whiskey. Would you like a cup of tea?"

He glowered in disgust. "A cup of tea? Now how in the hell is that going to help my eye? Do you at least have a couple of aspirin?"

"You're making a bigger fuss about this than you did when you broke your leg skiing a few years ago."

"Eleven years ago," he corrected her. "I was a lot younger then. My body could adapt to injury more easily. And I got a helluva lot more sympathy from—" He paused. "From the girl who was with me at the time than I'm getting from you!"

"Darla," said Brynn. "Darla Walsh. That's who you were with when you broke your leg skiing."

"Oh, yeah, I vaguely remember her."

"She thought you were in love with her," Brynn reminded him.

Sterne scowled. "Jeez, how do you remember all this stuff, anyway? It's my life and *I've* forgotten it."

Brynn shrugged. "I have a terrific memory for names and faces. I don't forget anyone I've met."

"Of course, I remember now. Stacey always would stand next to you at those stupid political receptions so you could tell her the names of everyone she'd previously met and forgotten." He managed a reminiscent smile. "Remember how much Stacey hated to go to those things? The folks would have to bribe, beg, and cajole her into it, and in the end she'd only go if you came along."

Brynn nodded. "Stacey loathes politics. It's fortunate that Justin agreed before they were married to resign from your father's campaign."

"Justin gave up a hell of a lot for her."

"You wouldn't. You've never put anyone else's feelings or wishes or happiness before your own. You're the most unconnected person I've ever known."

"You never miss a chance to zap me with one of your zingers, do you?" He frowned. "I'm not the selfish hedonist you make me out to be, Brynn. I'm just looking for happiness like everyone else. Doesn't the Declaration of Independence guarantee everyone the pursuit of happiness?"

"You have happiness confused with pleasure. Pleasure is a physical sensation that palls after a time. Happiness comes when you're living a productive life and are involved with other people."

"When I want a sermon, I'll go to church, thank you."

"That would be a novelty."

"That's it. I've had it." He sat up and tossed the icebag at her. She deftly caught it. "You're impossible! You're preachy and sarcastic and unsympathetic. Not to mention combative! I cross the street to avoid people like you, so what am I doing here?" He stormed into the kitchen and snatched his clothes, and pulled them on while he continued his tirade. "You say you want to get married? Well, you don't stand a chance of landing a man, you acid-tongued little shrew! You don't have what it takes to hold a man!"

"And you don't have what it takes to hold a woman," Brynn said calmly as she leaned against the door jamb, her arms folded as she watched him tug on his shirt and jeans.

"The hell I don't! I can get any woman I want into bed. Including you, sweetheart!"

"I wasn't talking about bed, I was talking about loving. You have sex and love hopelessly separated, Sterne Lipton. And you may be a successful sexual athlete, but you don't have what it takes to make a woman love you."

"Innumerable women have loved me! And probably still do," he replied coldly as he brushed past her.

"Name one."

He paused. The pause lengthened. Finally, he gave a slight laugh. "Your point, Brynnie. There isn't one—and that includes my stepmother and my sister."

Brynn was momentarily bewildered. Had she imagined the bleak shadow that had momentarily clouded his face? Or was she being set up? Sterne Lipton was manipulative enough to do it. Nevertheless, she was unable to keep from saying, "You know your mother and Stacey love you very much, Sterne."

"Stacey has tried," he conceded. "But I haven't let her get close enough. As for Caroline, she's not my mother. My father married her when I was six and Spence was four, just a year and a half after our real mother was killed in a hotel fire."

"Don't try to put any wicked stepmother stories over on me, Sterne. I've been around your family for fifteen years and I've seen how well your stepmother has treated you. She's been as nice to you as she's been to me."

He grinned wryly. "I did say you were unsympathetic, didn't I?"

"You're the one who warned Stacey and me to beware when a guy starts talking about his troubled childhood. You assured us it was merely an effective ploy a man uses to get a woman into the sack—one you'd used yourself with unfailing results!"

"A good memory is a curse in a woman," Sterne lamented mockingly.

Unexpectedly, they smiled at each other.

"This is the first time," Brynn said hesitantly, "I've ever heard anyone mention your . . . natural mother. Years after I met Stacey, I read in a magazine that Caroline was your father's second wife. I was so surprised. None of the Liptons had ever said anything about a previous marriage."

"It isn't discussed. It never has been. Grace McKellum, our housekeeper, broke the news of our mother's death to Spence and me. There was a private memorial service, and that was it. Our father never said a word about our mother to us then, and never has since. All of her things were removed from the house the day after she died. It was as though she'd never existed." He gave a self-deprecatory laugh. "I still have strong memories of her, but there were times when the silence was so pervasive I wondered if I'd merely dreamed her up."

Brynn stared at him. For the first time since she'd

known Sterne she saw beneath the cool rake's facade to the pain he sought to suppress. It shone in his eyes, radiating from deep within him. Genuine emotion was something one didn't see in Sterne Lipton. She held her breath, wondering what to say, what not to say. Sterne was so cynical. One wrong word and he'd close up and accuse her of sounding like a sentimental greeting card.

Her silence proved to be the most effective choice. Sterne continued to talk, his gaze unfocused, his voice holding a faraway note. "Grace gathered all the photographs of my mother and put them in a box for Spence and me and gave them to us when we were older. I didn't look at them for years, but lately, in the past year or so, I've found myself staring at them, wondering . . ." His voice trailed off. He looked troubled, confused.

"I'd like to see those pictures someday," Brynn said quietly. "Will you show them to me?"

He nodded absently. "She wasn't a classic beauty, like Caroline is, but in every one of those pictures, my mother—Dorothy Ann was her name—was laughing and animated and sparkling. She looked so alert, so alive. Even my dad looked human in those pictures with her. There wasn't a trace of the robotized political stiff he turned into. They looked so young, so happy."

"How old was your mother when she died?" Brynn asked softly.

"Twenty-nine. Dad was thirty. They'd been college sweethearts and married the day after my mother graduated from Nebraska State. From what I've pieced together, Mom had flown to Lincoln for the funeral of a friend's father and had planned to fly back that same day. But a snowstorm closed the airport, so she checked into one of the nearby hotels for the night. There was a fire, due to faulty electrical wiring. . . ." He shrugged. "I've seen the newspaper clippings. Thirteen people were killed in that fire, Dorothy Ann Lipton included."

"Oh, Sterne, it's so sad! Your father must have been devastated!"

"Yeah. Well, you don't have to worry about Bradford Lipton. No one does. He managed to put it all behind him quite swiftly and move on to other things. A new wife, new kids. A super-successful political career. I'm sure he felt it was just too bad that Spence and I were left behind as reminders of his old life."

Brynn was about to deny the harsh assertion automatically. Then she gazed into Sterne's dark blue eyes and remained silent. Whether it was true or not, Sterne believed it to be so. She ached for him. She knew quite well the pain of a parent's death, followed by the chilling rejection of the surviving parent, for she'd experienced it herself.

She'd lost her own mother when she was ten, then watched her father turn away from her in his grief. She had coped by turning to the Liptons and giving her love to a surrogate family. Sterne hadn't fared as well. He had internalized his pain and coped by avoiding love altogether.

Impulsively, she laid her hand on his arm. "I'm so sorry, Sterne." He could see the compassion in her light green eyes. He didn't want the demands and the complications of involvement with another person, but he had to admit that it felt *good* to know that Brynn cared enough to grieve for Dorothy Ann Lipton and the sons she'd left behind. And he could trust Brynn. She'd been around for years, she knew him as well as anyone ever had. All the Liptons knew that Brynn Cassidy wouldn't run to the nearest literary agent to sell the scoop of an inside look at life with the Lipton clan.

Brynn wanted to explore this new and unknown side of Sterne. "Caroline was very young when she married your father," she said, carefully steering the conversation. "Incredibly young to be a stepmother."

"She was twenty-one. It had to be hard on her, being stuck with a ready-made family at that age." Sterne grimaced. "Dad was always off politicking and then

Stacey and Lucas were born, and neither was the easiest kid to raise. Spence and I were even harder to deal with. Spence has always been kind of weird, and I was"—he grinned—"an obstreperous, obnoxious little monster."

She smiled at him, remembering when he'd flung those very words at her in his car last night. "Like me, hmm?"

"Yeah." He tweaked a strand of her straight auburn hair. "Like you."

"You couldn't help it. You missed your mother," she said softly. "As sweet and well-meaning as Caroline is, she couldn't take your mother's place."

"No, I never saw Caroline as a mother. Which made it damn awkward when I reached my teens. When I was thirteen, she was only twenty-eight. And feminine. And sexy. And beautiful. A living, breathing fantasy right in my own home. Do you get my drift?"

Brynn's eyes widened. "Sterne, you never tried to—"

"No," he interrupted with a laugh. "I never made a pass at my stepmother. But I turned my attentions elsewhere. I was bored with the giddy girls my age, and there were plenty of young women who weren't averse to initiating the senator's son into the delights of sexual pleasure. The folks weren't pleased, to say the least. Thus began my exile to a series of military schools."

"All of which you managed to get yourself kicked out of," Brynn added. She knew that particular bit of Lipton lore. "You finally got your high school diploma from a tough inner-city public high school in D.C."

"Good old Cardoza High. My boyish pranks didn't intimidate the administration there in the least. We had murderers, drug dealers, and pimps in the senior class. But hey, who's complaining? Then it was on to the good old University of Nebraska."

"Where you were president of your fraternity the year it was put on probation for hell-raising." Brynn knew that part of Lipton lore too. "Under your leadership, the house managed to get itself kicked permanently off campus."

"It was one of my campaign promises." He grinned. "*Animal House* had nothing on us. So, now you've heard about my troubled boyhood. Are you ready for bed?"

He was joking. His blue eyes were sparkling with laughter. Brynn laughed with him. He was outrageous and incorrigible, but for a few moments he'd let down his guard and she'd glimpsed a man she'd never encountered before. A man who wasn't self-involved and shallow, but one who had been hurt and had built walls against the pain. A man who could laugh at himself. A true narcissist was incapable of all of that.

Sterne stared down at her laughing face. Her eyes were glowing with warmth and humor. He felt . . . odd, connected to Brynn in a way he'd never experienced before with anyone else. They'd known each other for so long. She saw him—and through him—in a way that should have alarmed him, but didn't. It felt . . . comfortable.

He'd told her things he'd never vocalized before. He had never mentioned his mother and the pain of his loss to anyone. And he'd told Brynn about his adolescent crush on his stepmother, a secret he'd considered too shameful ever to reveal. Yet having discussed both the painful and the shameful, he felt neither pain nor shame. He felt . . . free? He instinctively knew he could talk to Brynn about anything at any time. No subject was taboo.

It was very strange, he mused. He could talk to her like a sister, yet when he took her into his arms, the feelings she evoked in him were as far from brotherly as they could possibly get. There was something special between them that he'd never known before.

Uh-oh! A warning bell sounded in his head. He'd lived within his self-protective shell for too long to cast it blindly aside and forge into the uncharted territory of emotional intimacy. Heaven save him from a meaningful relationship! He was a fun-loving, commitment-free bachelor, he reminded himself, and marriage-minded types like Brynn lived to alter his status.

She was already beginning to change her perceptions of him. He could see it in her eyes. She was prepared to be understanding. It was downright scary—he didn't want to be understood! He decided he preferred it when she called him a slug. It was safer. He hastily revised his assessment of their friendship. There was *nothing* special between them! He'd better make that immediately and unmistakably clear to her.

He frowned. He had to push her away, but how? Should he lapse into the role of insulting rake? No, he'd better not risk that again. The area around his eye was starting to throb and he didn't want to provoke her into another attack. The jocular big brother, then? Perfect.

"I've got to run, little sis," he said quickly, too quickly, and patted her head the way one might a small child's or a pet dog's. "I have a hot date tonight. Brunette with big brown eyes. Thirty-eight, twenty-four, thirty-four. Indescribably delicious."

It was a stunning retreat. Brynn could do nothing but stare at Sterne. One moment, they'd been laughing together, feeling close, on the verge of . . . what? She wasn't sure, but she knew that the opportunity to find out was irretrievably lost. Sterne was back to being the man whose depth didn't reach superficial. The lover, the playboy, the rake. Disappointment coursed through her. She looked at him and said nothing.

He went on. "Sorry about the way things turned out with your Doctor Prince, honey. Tell you what. I'll make a play for the girl who got her hooks into him. What's her name? I'll call her tomorrow and have her in the sack by tomorrow night. Then you can console the doc. Hey, don't thank me. What are surrogate big brothers for?"

"'I don't want Daniel King on the rebound and I don't

want you to seduce Nicolette on my behalf," Brynn replied coolly. She knew very well that Sterne was regretting those brief moments when he'd confided in her. Yet having been in communication with Sterne Lipton, the human being, however fleetingly, she was finding it irritatingly difficult to have to go back to dealing with Sterne Lipton, the sexually-obsessed humanoid.

"No?" He shrugged. "You're the one who's lusting after a wedding ring, honey. I was just trying to do you a favor."

"I am not lusting after a wedding ring. And when and if I do get married, it'll be without any favors from you, you slug."

Sterne grinned. He was back on safe ground. " 'Bye, Brynnie. See you around." It was his traditional leave-taking. He'd been saying it to her for years.

"Oh, I hope not." It was her traditional parting shot. She'd been saying it to him for years.

Brynn heard him whistling as he bounded down the steps of the apartment building. The strange interlude between them was over. She should be feeling relieved. Sterne Lipton spelled trouble to any woman. No one knew that better than she.

Sterne bolted from the building and into the rain, which was still falling heavily from the gray skies. He didn't mind getting wet. It was refreshing and revitalizing. Strange, but that's how he felt, refreshed and revitalized and oddly lighthearted. He didn't understand it, but it was a stunning contrast to the enervating ennui that normally engulfed him. He thought ahead to his date with the brunette, Lila something. Or was it Linda? Unlike Brynn, he was terrible with names.

Brynnie. The image of her face, soft and pretty, her green eyes alive with laughter, flashed into his mind and he felt a knifelike thrust in his loins. Immediately he blocked the image and the shaft of desire. He felt nothing, he insisted to himself. Nothing.

By the time he arrived back at his apartment, the Secret Service men dutifully following in their black sedan, he felt restless and out of sorts. By the time his luscious companion for the evening arrived at his apartment wearing a black peek-a-boo teddy and nothing else under her raincoat, he was bored beyond measure.

Five

When Brynn walked into Sterne's Place in Georgetown two weeks later, Sterne didn't question the sudden, sharp stab of pleasure he felt at the sight of her. He got up from the bar stool where he was halfheartedly romancing a bosomy blonde and approached Brynn, who looked both sweet and sexy in a canary-yellow sundress that emphasized the soft curve of her breasts and her slender waist. The full skirt swirled around her long, well-shaped legs. Her auburn hair swung loose and silky around her shoulders. She hadn't seen him yet, and he quickened his stride.

Then he saw her turn, animated and laughing, to the man behind her—whose hand rested possessively on her waist! She'd come here with a date! Sterne froze and ducked behind the bar, his gaze flicking speculatively over the other man. Not too tall, medium build, regular features. Neatly, but not very stylishly dressed. Sterne's mouth curved into a derisive frown. The guy was probably fresh from the Midwest. Sterne knew the type well. The University of Nebraska had been filled with them. Nice, normal, marriageable men. Unconsciously, instinctively, he clenched his jaw.

"Well, here we are," Brynn said to her date as she smiled up at him. "See any celebrities?" She hadn't wanted to come to Sterne's Place tonight, but Robert was new in the city and eager to see the President's son's bar, the very one he'd seen featured on television.

Robert Layne was from Omaha and a devoted admirer of his fellow Nebraskan, Bradford Lipton. He found the idea of being near anything remotely connected with any Lipton incredibly exciting. Brynn suspected that her status as Lipton family friend was what had prompted Robert to ask her out in the first place, but this was their second date and she found him a pleasant and undemanding companion.

They'd been to a movie tonight, and when Robert had suggested a nightcap at Sterne's Place, Brynn had stifled her initial objections and decided to indulge him. After all, it was the end of June. Sterne was undoubtedly spending the weekend in Rehoboth Beach, happily hunting among the singles who flocked there. Anyway, it was common knowledge that he spent less and less time at his bars. The odds on his being at Sterne's Place tonight were about a million to one.

"Well, well, look who's here." Seemingly from nowhere, Sterne Lipton materialized before them. "It's a real surprise to see you here tonight, Brynnie."

Brynn suppressed a groan. A million to one odds and she'd lost! "Hi, Sterne." She forced a smile. He was stylishly dressed in pastels, à la *Miami Vice*, and was tanned and tall and unbelieveably handsome. He totally eclipsed nice, average Robert, and was fully aware of it.

"It *is* a surprise meeting you here tonight," she added with more of an edge than she'd intended. Surprises were sometimes unpleasant, and she had an uneasy feeling that this surprise fell into that category. Nor did she care for the way Sterne was looking at Robert—like a shark sizing up a swimmer at the beach.

Sterne grinned at her. "I thought about going to Rehoboth this weekend but decided to stay in town. You know, give the tourists a thrill." He winked conspiratorially at Robert, who smiled broadly, obviously overwhelmed to be acknowledged by a bona fide celebrity.

Brynn swallowed. "Robert, this is Sterne Lipton, as you probably know. Sterne, this is Robert Layne. He's from Omaha." She moved closer to Robert and laid a protective hand on his arm. She didn't trust the wolflike gleam in those dark blue eyes of Sterne's. Sterne, like all the Lipton offspring, was normally aloof with strangers. The fact that he had draped his arm around Robert's shoulder and was greeting him like a long-lost fraternity brother did not bode well.

"Robert from Omaha?" he said. "Hey, it's a great city, huh? D.C. doesn't have anything on our good old Omaha! So, Robert, what brings you to Washington? Have a drink, on the house, and fill me in on the news back home. Is that cute brunette still reading the weather reports on Channel Six?"

"Oh, yes. Yes, thanks!" Robert was overwhelmed by Sterne's display of friendliness. Brynn's nerves tightened. What was Sterne up to? She watched him sweep Robert away from her, seating him at the bar with a flourish. She pushed her way through the crowd, which was ogling the President's son and his new friend.

At the bar, Robert was being treated to a free drink. "I was transferred here two months ago," Brynn heard him tell Sterne. "I'm with Mutual Insurance. I met Brynn at church," he added, casting a smile in her direction.

"At church," Sterne repeated flatly. Robert Layne, so nice, so normal, so *marriageable*. He'd met Brynn at church. Sterne was suddenly filled with an inexplicable cold rage that wiped out the apathy he'd been feeling since leaving Brynn's apartment two endless weeks ago.

He leaned forward and said something to Robert in a voice so low, he couldn't be overheard. By the time

Brynn had jostled her way to their side, Robert was staring at her as if she were a cobra with two heads.

Stern slipped from his bar stool. "Order yourself whatever you want, Brynnie. It's on the house, of course." He nodded to Robert, gave his shoulder a fraternal pat, and walked away.

"Good night, Brynn," Robert Layne said as he backed away from her at her apartment door.

Brynn mustered a smile. "Would you like to come in for coffee? I know it's eighty degrees outside, but I have iced coffee if you prefer."

"No!" Robert said quickly. "I have to—to . . . uh, leave. Now. Good-bye."

Brynn stared at him, disconcerted. Robert had barely spoken to her since they'd left Sterne's Place. And he kept backing away from her whenever she came within two feet of him. When she'd tried to take his arm to cross the street, he'd jerked away as though she were radioactive.

"What did Sterne say to you?" Brynn blurted out, and by the flush that stained Robert's cheeks, she knew she'd hit upon the right clue to his inexplicable withdrawal.

"Look, I—er—it's—uh—" Robert lapsed into total incoherence. "Let's just call it a night, Brynn."

He never intended to call her again, she realized. He would cross the street to avoid her, if necessary. She could see it in his wild-eyed expression. But why? "Robert, I feel I have a right to know what Sterne said, since it obviously concerns me."

Robert swallowed hard. "I'm not condemning you, Brynn. It's just that I . . . Well, I don't want to have to deal with that . . . er, particular pr-problem."

"What particular problem?"

He looked at his shoes. "Herpes," he muttered, his face scarlet. "Sterne told me you have it."

Brynn went rigid with shock. Then she went blind,

deaf, and mute with sheer fury. "Sterne told you that, about me?" she managed to ask at last after several seconds of stunned, enraged silence.

But Robert was already halfway down the stairs. He was a nice, normal, marriageable man who wasn't up to coping with these sophisticated eastern career women. Had Sterne told him that she was deranged, Robert might have attempted to be understanding. But a disease he associated with sexual liberation? He couldn't get away from her fast enough!

"It's not true!" she shouted down the stairwell. But Robert had already left the building. He wasn't about to stick around for explanations.

Sterne had gauged the other man's reaction well and said exactly the right words to speed him on his way, Brynn thought as she seethed with rage. But why had he done it? Why? Then it struck her. His motive was revenge, pure and simple. He hadn't forgiven her for taking his car and leaving it at the airport, nor for that smack she'd given him. It had taken two weeks, but he'd avenged himself.

She pictured him, sitting on a bar stool, surrounded by admiring cuties while he basked in the glow of his revenge. She imagined his smug smile of satisfaction and her temper erupted with volcanic intensity.

Her hands shaking, she looked up the number of Sterne's Place in the telephone directory and dialed it. One of the bartenders told her that Sterne had left the bar.

"With a woman, I presume?" she asked with what she hoped was a breezy insouciance.

The bartender chuckled. "When doesn't Sterne leave with a woman?"

"When, indeed?" Brynn replaced the receiver. If he'd left with a woman, he was inevitably heading to that libertine's lair he called his apartment. She flexed her fingers. *Well, Sterne Lipton,* she thought, *you're not getting away with this one.*

Too furious even to begin to think clearly, her common sense obliterated by indignant rage, Brynn stalked from her apartment. Her trusty old car, a Chevy Nova, seemed to drive itself through the city traffic. When she pulled up in front of Sterne's apartment complex, she could hardly remember how she'd gotten there. Certainly, her mind hadn't been on her driving. It had been wholly on Sterne Lipton.

A Secret Service agent stopped her on the fifteenth floor as she walked toward Sterne's apartment. "I'm Brynn Cassidy," she told him. "And I'm going in there. Don't try to stop me."

"Jack Rivington," the agent replied. "I was at the window of the Maserati when you took off in it a couple weeks back. Spent half the next day in the rain helping Sterne look for it. Pleased to meet you at last, Miss Cassidy," he added cordially. "I'm assigned to Sterne Lipton."

"You might be out of a job, Mr. Rivington. I'm here to take Sterne Lipton apart, piece by loathsome piece."

Rivington took her purse and searched it briefly but thoroughly before handing it back to her. "You don't have any concealed weapons on you, Miss Cassidy. I suppose I can let you go in. But I feel I ought to warn you. Sterne brought a woman home with him."

"She'll be out of there in two minutes flat." Brynn's eyes were flashing green fire. "I don't want any witnesses to the mayhem I'm about to commit."

Rivington hid a smile and walked her to the door of Sterne's apartment. She pounded on it, then rang the bell without letting up until they heard Sterne's voice calling from within, "All right! All right! I'm coming!"

"Who is it?" asked lovely blonde Gloria. Or was it Gina? Sterne wondered. He made a mental note to ask her name again. Not that it mattered. He was in a terrible mood. Perhaps he would use the pounding at the door as an excuse to send her on her way.

"Probably one of the Secret Service agents," he replied indifferently. He opened the door, ignoring the fact that he was wearing only a large blue bath towel that covered him from waist to knee. His hair was damp, and he'd just stepped out of the shower.

"You have company, Sterne," Rivington announced unnecessarily; Brynn had already pushed inside.

"Brynn!" Sterne gasped at the sight of her. Adrenaline poured into his system in a heated rush. Suddenly, he was alive. The deadening apathy had been blown away by her appearance.

"Get dressed and go home," Brynn told Gloria/Gina tautly. "I have private business with Sterne."

The blonde, wrapped in one of Sterne's thigh-length silk robes, glanced at him in confusion.

"He'll give you cab fare," Brynn said. "Believe me, you don't want to be here for this."

"I think you'd better do as Miss Cassidy says," Rivington advised. "I'll call a taxi for you."

Sterne gazed from Rivington to Gina/Gloria to Brynn. "What's going on here?" he demanded.

Brynn's control, tenuous at best, snapped. She whirled on him. "You bastard! I could kill you. I am going to kill you—with Mr. Rivington's blessing!" She started toward him, advancing on him with the determination of a predatory cat stalking its helpless, hapless prey.

To his everlasting humiliation, Sterne began to back away from her. The bruise around his eye had been blue and purple before fading to a sickly yellow-green. Rivington and the other agent had grinned knowingly whenever he'd explained to acquaintances that he'd walked into a door. All traces of it had faded now, and he did not care to acquire another one.

"This time you've gone too far!" Brynn picked up a lucite bookend and threw it at him. Then she picked up a book and threw it too.

Sterne caught both, but didn't set either back down. He had a strong feeling they'd be hurled right back at him if he did.

"I think I *will* go," the blonde said nervously. She grabbed her clothes and tucked them under her arm. Still wearing Sterne's robe, she left the apartment, gallantly escorted by Rivington. The door closed behind them.

"How could you?" Brynn snatched up an open bottle of champagne from a chrome ice bucket. "How dare you tell such a filthy lie about me?"

Sterne watched her warily. She was going to hit him with the bottle. He knew it. He was aware that he fully deserved it, but winced in anticipated pain nevertheless. "Brynn, calm down." He tried to make his voice soft and soothing. It occurred to him that he'd never seen anyone so angry in his entire life. "I . . . uh, can explain."

"No, you can't! There is no justifiable explanation for what you did. You slandered me! I ought to sue you! I would, except it would only hurt your family and they've been hurt enough, being related to a self-centered sub-human creep like you!"

Sterne swallowed. "You have every right to be upset," he said tentatively.

"You're damn right I do. I met Robert at church! What if he decides to spread what you said around the congregation?" Her hands were shaking so violently that champagne sloshed out of the bottle, over her fingers and onto the white shag rug.

Sterne cleared his throat. "Brynn . . ."

She saw him through a haze of red. Had the bottle of champagne been a firearm, she would have pulled the trigger. "I hate you! I've never hated anyone more in my whole life! Your mother was lucky she didn't live to see what a selfish, useless, wicked man you grew up to be!"

There was a moment of charged silence. The red mist cleared. Brynn burst into tears.

The champagne bottle slipped from her fingers and noiselessly hit the rug. Sterne stared at Brynn, whose face was buried in her hands. He'd never seen her cry before, not ever. He knew she wasn't the type to cry easily, to turn the tears on and off like a faucet as some women did. She was really hurt. The feelings creeping through him were entirely new to him. He felt lower than the lowest lowlife. He had hurt her and made her cry. He *was* lower than the lowest lowlife.

"Brynn." He took a hesitant step toward her. He was feeling alternately hot and cold. He didn't know what to say or do. "Please don't cry."

It wasn't as if he hadn't seen a woman's tears before. Of course he had. Normally, he merely detached himself and observed the rather interesting spectacle of running mascara, which invariably gave the weeper a raccoonlike appearance.

But watching Brynn cry . . . damn, it was terrible. She looked so small, like a hurt, lost child. Pain seared him. He couldn't detach himself, he couldn't take his eyes from her. He had done this to her.

"I shouldn't have said it," she managed to whisper on a breathless sob. "It was unspeakably cruel. Can you ever forgive me?"

Sterne gaped at her. "Me? Forgive you? For what?"

She dropped her hands and looked at him. Her eyes were red, her nose puffy. Tears streaked her cheeks. Her mascara had run, but she didn't look like a raccoon. She looked . . . fragile. Vulnerable. Lovable. Sterne caught his breath.

"For what I said about your mother," she whispered. "I didn't mean it, Sterne. I—I wanted to hurt you, but . . ." A fresh flood of tears threatened. "I don't know how I could've said anything so heartless! I'm so sorry, Sterne."

"I deserved it," he said finally. He was baffled. He had thought she was crying because of what he'd told Robert Layne in the bar. *That* had been unspeakable. Cruel. Unforgivable. So why was *she* asking *his* forgiveness?

Because she'd said that his mother was lucky that she hadn't lived to see what kind of a man her son had become? That was the truth. What had he ever done to make anyone proud of him? He didn't care about anything or anyone, and nothing and no one cared about him.

It was the first time he'd ever made that admission to himself. He was profoundly jarred by it. "You were absolutely right, you know," he said quietly. "The truth always hurts. And I had it coming."

"I lost my mother too. I know what it's like." Brynn was calmer now, her voice husky and filled with remorse. "There are some things that should be strictly off-limits in a fight, and mothers—especially mothers who've died—are one of them. I deliberately went for the jugular with that remark and I apologize."

Sterne sucked in his breath. She was making him feel worse and worse. He knew he was a cad, but he'd never felt like one until now. "If anyone should be apologizing, it's me. Telling Layne what I did was totally rotten. I'll call him in the morning and tell him it isn't true." He ran a hand through his damp hair tousling it. "I don't know why in the hell I said it, anyway," he added, not meeting her eyes.

"I do." She stooped to pick up the champagne bottle. A small puddle of the cold liquid was seeping into the rug. "You wanted to get back at me for taking your car."

"Is that what you think?" He knew she was dead wrong. Although he refused to acknowledge what had motivated him to drive a wedge between Brynn and that nice, normal, marriageable man she'd met at church, he was well aware that the car-napping had nothing to do with it. A chill ran through him. Maybe it was better to let her think she was right.

He shrugged. "I'm sorry." It was difficult to say. He seldom bothered with apologies. There was seldom anything he wanted to set to rights. "I told you I'd call Layne and I will."

She managed a small smile. "Not that I'd ever go out with *him* again, even if he begged me to. What a judgmental, intolerant prig he turned out to be! Suppose what you told him had been the truth? His reaction was way out of line. He had no right to treat me as if I was slime from the garbage heap."

Sterne winced. It bothered him to think of anyone treating her that way. Yet he'd anticipated just such a reaction from Layne, hadn't he? His head swam with confusion. Was he starting to lose his sanity, or what? He glanced wildly around the room, and his gaze lit on the champagne bottle she was holding. "Do you want some champagne?" He needed something to dull his brain and keep his thoughts at bay. He took the bottle from her and looked around for two glasses.

Brynn shook her head. "I'm going home now. I'll tell Rivington that his charge is unharmed."

"He'll be disappointed. Rivington thoroughly disapproves of me." Sterne paused. "Not that I blame him. There isn't much about me to admire, is there, Brynnie?"

"There could be," she said softly.

A wave of tenderness washed over him. Only doggedly loyal Brynnie could say that. He had a feeling she would never give up on him, no matter how much he might infuriate her. He knew he didn't deserve that kind of loyalty, and yet he realized he liked having it, from her.

They looked at each other for a long, silent moment. Brynn felt a knot of tension tightening within her. For the first time since she'd burst into his apartment, she became aware that Sterne was clad only in a towel. Her gaze slid over his broad shoulders, the muscular arms, the hair on his chest. His fingers were moving back and forth over the champagne bottle. They were long fingers, sensuous, experienced.

She gulped. "Well . . . um, I'll be going now. I probably have half a dozen parking tickets on my car by now. I parked illegally, in front of the building in the loading zone."

"If you do, give them to me and I'll have them taken care of. I have a special arrangement with the management."

"I'm sure." The management was probably a woman, willing and curvaceous, like the blonde she'd sent packing earlier. Brynn's mouth tightened. "Good-bye, Sterne." She turned and started toward the door.

His hand snaked out and grabbed her wrist. "Before you go, don't you want a guided tour of the place? The bathroom has been customized and is quite a showplace."

"I'll bet," she said dryly. "Then there's your infamous bedroom. . . . Let me guess. You have a full sound system, a TV and VCR to show your collection of blue movies, specially installed soft lighting, and a king-sized waterbed. With zebra-striped satin sheets on it."

"Leopard-skin satin sheets," he corrected her. "The zebra-striped ones are at the dry cleaners." He furrowed his brow. "How did you know about the zebra sheets, anyway? And how do you know about the sound system and the lighting and the movies and the waterbed? Did someone tell you? Stacey, perhaps?"

"Stacey never got as far as your bedroom. Remember the bathtub incident? No, I just guessed. Everything I mentioned seemed likely tools of the trade for a professional rake."

Professional rake. He'd been called worse, but for some reason, at this particular moment, the term set his teeth on edge. "I suppose you have virginal white cotton sheets on that virginal single bed of yours."

She shrugged. "What else would a virgin have?" The moment the words were out of her mouth, she wanted to recall them. Her virgin status was her deepest, innermost secret. And she'd just blurted it out—to Sterne Lipton, of all people! A hot, slow blush suffused her face, from her neck to the roots of her hair.

Sterne was staggered. He stared at her, his jaw agape. "You—you're—you mean you're . . ." He paused to draw a breath. "You mean you're like a—a—" He swallowed. "A virgin?"

"Just like the song," she said wryly. "Only I'm not *like* one, I *am* one."

"I don't believe it!" His gaze swept over her compulsively, again and again. "You've always had plenty of dates. You almost got engaged to that guy you dated in college, didn't you? The tall, blond turkey with the bulging pectorals?"

"Mark Harcourt. He wasn't a turkey and I didn't sleep with him."

"No, according to you, you've never slept with anyone!" Sterne felt shaken. He wondered at the unfamiliar sense of protectiveness that was surging through him as he gazed at her slender, supple body. It was alarming and inexplicable. So was this totally incomprehensible possessiveness that was rushing over him as his gaze strayed compulsively to her wide green eyes, her soft mouth. He'd never experienced either before. It was easier to understand the strong urge to run away, to hop into his Maserati and put a thousand miles between him and his green-eyed nemesis.

As the internal conflict raged he was aware that he felt as far removed from his usual numbing apathy as he'd ever been in his life.

"Well, now you know," Brynn said. She walked toward the door. "I'd appreciate it if you'd refrain from telling my dates." She cast him a thin smile. "It might scare them off quicker than herpes."

Which brought them back to what he'd done. Somehow, in light of this new revelation, it seemed a million times worse. Sterne groaned. "Lord, Brynnie, I'm sorry!" If there was a hell, he was headed there for sure. And rightly so.

He couldn't take his eyes off her. He stared at the delicate curve of her neck, the vulnerable nape, and at the tempting curve of her breasts, and the gentle flare of her hips. He drew in a long, harsh breath. She'd never had a man. If he—if they— His brain clouded. Disjointed thoughts tumbled through his mind. He could be the first. He'd never thought about it before with anyone, but he found that he loved the idea.

Brynn caught him gazing at her and frowned. "Stop staring at me that way." He'd once said the same thing to her, she recalled, and blushed.

"Which way?" he asked huskily.

"Like I'm a steak dinner you're set on devouring."

He laughed. "That's hardly an apt analogy, baby. Uh, Brynn," he corrected himself. "Sorry, I know you don't like to be called baby. I'll try to remember not to do it."

She glanced at him sharply. Sterne was making an effort to consider her wishes? And the way he was watching her . . . Her eyes narrowed with suspicion. "*Now* what are you up to?"

."Me? Nothing! Nothing at all." He shook his head. He was at war with himself. One part demanded that he run from her and stay as far away as he possibly could. The other part urged him to take her in his arms and kiss her soft mouth, to caress her until she was sighing and clinging to him. . . .

They were at the door and Brynn had her hand on the lock, ready to unbolt it and leave. "Why, Brynnie?" Sterne's voice, low and deep and husky, stopped her in her tracks. "Why haven't you ever had a lover?"

She stared at the ground. "I don't know. Maybe because I've never been in love and, as you said, I have love and sex hopelessly linked." Her lips curved into a self-mocking smile. "I never set out to save myself for the man I married, not consciously, anyway. I suppose you're going to accuse me of that, though."

"Lover and husband are not synonymous terms to me, honey."

"How true." She smiled. "Maybe they are to me, I don't know. Or maybe I'm just as leery of commitment and deep emotional involvement as you are. Except you choose to avoid it by overindulging sexually while I avoid it by abstaining."

"I've never been one for introspection and self-analysis." He stepped closer and smoothed her hair from her face. "Whatever the reason . . ." His voice trailed off as he gazed into the pale green depths of her eyes. He lost his train of thought completely when her lips parted and she drew in a quick, shaky breath.

His hands threaded through her hair and he gently

pulled her head up to his. He massaged her scalp with his fingertips as he kissed either side of her mouth, quick, staccato kisses. Then his tongue slowly, sensuously, traced the outline of her lips.

Brynn didn't move. She knew she had to push him away, but when her hands went to do so, they ignored her mind's order and rested on his waist instead. The roughness of his towel beneath her palms was a delicious contrast to his warm, smooth skin. If she were to spread her fingers out, she would encounter the dark path of wiry hair, another intriguing contrast to explore.

"Kiss me," Sterne said urgently. His gaze roamed her face before coming to rest hungrily on her mouth. "I want to feel your tongue in my mouth."

Her pulse jumped. "Sterne . . ."

"Kiss me!"

One moment they were a step apart, staring at each other, and the next they were locked in each other's arms. Her mouth opened under his the moment their lips met, and Sterne groaned with satisfaction as his tongue penetrated the soft moistness within.

The kiss deepened hotly. His breathing was fast and shallow; he was taut and hard against her. Her body began to tremble. It softened and flowed, molding itself to his. Her legs felt rubbery and weak. She had a strong urge to lie down, to feel his warm weight upon her.

His hands cupped her breasts, and she couldn't suppress the soft moan that escaped from her throat when his fingers teased her nipples through the soft yellow cotton of her dress. They tightened into achingly sensitive peaks, and she cried out softly with pleasure. Her moan seemed to echo in Sterne's head, driving him on with sensual urgency. Brynn felt him shudder with desire, and she smoothed her hands over his muscular back.

Through a haze of sexual excitement, she felt his fingers deftly lowering the zipper of her sundress. It was a slow process, for he paused every few inches to caress the newly exposed skin.

"Let me have you," he said hoarsely, his body tight and throbbing against hers. He eased the narrow straps of her sundress from her shoulders. "I want you so much."

It was true, he realized, and was astonished by the revelation. This time he wasn't merely saying the words by rote; he actually meant them. When was the last time he'd felt this burning hunger, this deep *need*? Sexual desire had become merely an itch to him, and sex with a woman—any woman—simply scratched that itch on the surface. Sex was trivial, a meaningless physical exercise. But now, with Brynn . . .

It was so different. Kissing her, touching her, feeling her body shiver with response, it was all new with her. His head spun. His jaded senses were suddenly alert and alive with feeling and sensation. Not once did he forget who he was holding in his arms. This was Brynnie, and she was interchangeable with no one else. He had feelings for her that spanned the years. She aroused strong emotions in him, both positive and negative, which he simply couldn't blunt. And as he held her in his arms, every fiber of his being was filled with the primal knowledge that she belonged to him.

He lifted her up and slid her down the hard length of his body, then pressed her intimately against him, letting her know the full measure of his need. A wild, electric pleasure shot through Brynn, and she arched into him, moving sinuously, instinctively, in a primitive rhythm. She trembled and burned as she felt his burgeoning strength hot and hard between her legs.

She'd never felt such intense, sensual pleasure, and the sheer magnitude of it frightened her. No one had ever made her come so close to losing all control. Her eyes flew open, and she jerked away from Sterne.

He was no longer simply her best friend's fascinatingly irritating older brother with whom she was comfortably— albeit ambivalently—familiar. She saw him through a stranger's eyes, and those eyes saw a handsome and dangerous man who fairly radiated sexual energy. A man who lured and challenged a woman to surrender to that intense masculine heat. And if she chose to do so, it would be at her own risk.

Brynn gave her head a slight shake, as if to clear it. No, she told herself. Not her. Not after years and years of observing Sterne's throwaway attitude toward his lovers. She zipped up her dress, turned, and unbolted the door.

He caught her arm. "Don't be afraid, Brynnie," he said huskily. "I'm not going to hurt you."

"No, you're not." Her laugh was sad. "Because I'm not going to let you."

"You want me!" His voice was rough. The last time he'd made that proclamation it had sounded like an accusation, but not this time. This time he wanted her to want him, the way he wanted her. His fingers began to stroke the soft inner skin of her arm. "And I want you. We both need it, Brynn."

"That isn't good enough for me. It's never been before and it isn't now."

"Brynn, I want you badly, but I won't marry you just to get you into bed," he said harshly.

"You certainly won't! If there were ever an unlikely candidate for a husband, he would have to be you."

"And that's what you want, isn't it, honey? A nice, normal, marriageable guy. It isn't me, Brynnie. I'm just not a marrying man."

"We agree on that much, at least," she said dryly. Her common sense mercifully had been restored. Whatever sensual spell Sterne had cast over her had been broken, and she was back to her levelheaded self. Her levelheaded virginal self, she amended wryly. Despite Sterne's earlier mocking accusations, she'd never believed that it was possible to lose oneself to passion, to be swept away on the impulse of the moment. Until Sterne had taken her into his arms. . . .

"Good night, Sterne." She turned and walked out the door.

Sterne wanted to stop her. His whole body was aching with unfulfilled needs, and he was unaccustomed to dealing with frustration, particularly sexual frustration. "There's a name for hot little teases like you," he said in an attempt to work up a little self-serving and self-righteous anger, but even he had to concede that his heart wasn't in it. "Sexy little teases who send out signals, but don't deliver," he added lamely.

Who was he kidding? he asked himself. She was the innocent, and he'd been attempting to seduce her. Teasing hadn't come into it. Her response had been genuine, passionate, and uncontrolled. Heat swept through him as he remembered. It was exciting to think that he was making her feel things she'd never felt with a man. But his sense of masculine power was quickly supplanted by stronger feelings of protectiveness and . . . tenderness?

He was shaken by the force and unfamiliarity of these previously unawakened emotions surging through him. Impulsively, he stepped out into the hall and called after her. "Brynnie."

Brynn was already halfway down the hall to the elevator, but she paused and looked around at Sterne. The sight of him standing there, tall and tousled and pure male, clad only in the blue towel, struck a sensitive chord deep within her. Something primitive and long suppressed yearned and ached inside her, urging her to go to him, to touch him, to have him. But she didn't dare. Brynn knew herself well enough to realize that she couldn't go to Sterne lightly, couldn't indulge in one of the brief, hot flings for which he was noted, and emerge unscathed.

She shivered. No, she could never stand idly by and watch Sterne with other women once she'd given herself to him.

So . . . Brynn tore her eyes from Sterne and proceeded to the elevator without a word. It never occurred to her to consider the possibility of a fling with Sterne leading to anything other than pain and disaster for her. She knew as well as anyone that Sterne Lipton was not a marrying man.

Six

When Caroline Lipton called Brynn to invite her to the Liptons' summer house in Rehoboth Beach for a family celebration of the President's birthday over the Fourth of July weekend, Brynn accepted at once. Since the age of twelve, she'd spent every Fourth of July celebrating Bradford Lipton's birthday with his family at their beach house. Occasionally, Bradford Lipton himself actually made it to the festivities.

"The whole family will be there this year, Brynnie," Caroline said happily. "Stacey and Justin and the twins, Spence and Patty and the children, Lucas, and even Sterne has agreed to come."

"Terrific." Brynn managed to utter the reply that the older woman expected to hear, but she did not share Caroline Lipton's joyful anticipation. Sterne would be there. She hadn't seen him since she'd left his apartment last week in a haze of confusion. But she'd thought about him—way too much.

She thought about him during the day in her small office in the House Office Building where the Human

Resources Committee was headquartered, as she researched and wrote reports on the need for corporate-sponsored day-care centers, senior citizens' volunteer programs, and other proposals to solve current social problems. Since her friendship with the Lipton family was well known, her status on the committee had escalated once Bradford Lipton was elected president. She was considered a valuable contact with an open line to the powers-that-be.

But even as she delved into her projects, Sterne would slip insidiously into her thoughts. She would remember the way he'd looked, wrapped in the blue towel as he stood in the hallway outside his apartment, huskily calling her back to him.

It was even worse at night. Just looking at the pristine white sheets on her bed conjured up Sterne's stunned reaction to her virginity. Oh, how she regretted blurting that out! And as she lay on that narrow bed, other images—of water beds and leopard print sheets—flashed involuntarily before her mind's eye. She pictured Sterne lying on the bed, smiling that sexy, devilish smile of his, his dark blue eyes gleaming wickedly as he taunted her for her inexperience and challenged her to learn all about what she was missing . . . learn all about it with him.

The night Caroline Lipton called, Brynn found it impossible to sleep. She rolled over onto her stomach and buried her face in her pillow. Her breasts hurt. They were swollen, and her nipples were hard, tight points of sensitivity. Closing her eyes, she could recapture the feeling of Sterne's hands on her. His fingers had teased her nipples, circling them, rubbing them until she moaned with the pleasure he evoked.

She gritted her teeth and tried to think of the linear graphs and statistics pertaining to the committee's latest investigations, in order to suppress the images and feelings coursing through her. It didn't work. Her body pulsed and throbbed, and Brynn groaned aloud.

This temporary physical infatuation would pass, she

assured herself as she twisted the sheets around her. But how was she going to get through the weekend, sharing a house with Sterne, without any of the Liptons noticing that she was . . . well, practically in heat? She blushed at the analogy.

Abruptly sitting up in bed, Brynn switched on the lamp and reached for her crossword puzzle magazine. She would *not* spend another night in adolescent yearning for Sterne Lipton! She would survive the weekend by successfully playing the role she'd always played with Sterne, that of the sexually unaware and totally unsusceptible-to-his-charms kid sister. None of the Liptons would have to know of her temporary lapse of sanity, and perhaps by the end of the weekend she would have put things back in their proper perspective.

Fervently hoping that would be the case, Brynn pondered a nine-letter word meaning "opponent."

On Friday, the second of July, Sterne left for Rehoboth Beach, Delaware, in the early morning hours, well in advance of the heavy weekend traffic that would clog the bridges and highways leading to the shore. The rest of the family—and Brynn—had planned to arrive the evening before.

Unlike his sister and brothers, Sterne had his own condominium in the resort town and seldom stayed at the Liptons' sprawling beach house. Sterne's frenetic social life did not lend itself to communal family living. But this weekend, he had agreed to his stepmother's suggestion that he stay with the family. He didn't allow himself to consider why.

"We'll have more time with you if you stay at the house," Caroline had said with her usual tact. She never alluded to his lifestyle and the embarrassment it caused the nation's conservative chief executive. Caroline, as Brynn had pointed out, had always been nice to him. Too nice, perhaps, Sterne mused. Maybe he'd needed to be told a few home truths back in his wild days. Maybe he needed to hear those old home truths now.

His lips twisted into a grimace. Brynn was always willing to supply home truths. Tact didn't enter into it. She'd never been hesitant about ripping apart his character—or lack of it.

Brynn. Sterne frowned. The little fiend was haunting him. She'd been doing so all week. There didn't seem to be anything he could do to drive her out of his head. His mind wandered when he was with other women, so he made up excuses and sent his would-be lovers on their way.

He had to have something to fill the hours, so he went to his tiny office in the back of Sterne's Place and worked on the books. They were in appalling disorder and he felt a genuine sense of satisfaction when he'd finally systematically categorized everything with a clarity that would have pleased even the IRS. No one with the IQ of a clam could've handled that job, he told himself, and almost called Brynn to gloat.

But he didn't. Because he wanted to, too much. He was forever coming up with excuses to call her. Then, he would mentally enact their conversations. Anyone would think he'd become obsessed with her.

And he wasn't, Sterne insisted to himself. When he saw her this weekend, it would be like all the other times they'd spent together with his family. He wouldn't view her as a woman at all. She would simply be Brynnie, his sister's ever-present pal. The kid who'd swooned over rock stars and worried about getting a date to the prom. He didn't allow himself to picture her as any older than fifteen.

Sterne was a master at deluding himself, and by the time he arrived at the Liptons' huge frame house on the beach, he almost expected to see a teenaged Brynn and Stacey sitting on the wide front porch swing, sipping sodas and giggling.

Instead, he saw his twenty-seven-year-old sister and

her equally mature friend tending Stacey's two-year-old twins.

"Hi, Sterne!" Stacey called to him, and waved. She and Brynn were both wearing bathing suits and sitting in lawn chairs. Beside them was the small plastic pool where little Amanda and Allison Marks were gleefully splashing.

Sterne forced himself to walk nonchalantly over to them. "It's so good to see you!" Stacey exclaimed, giving him a fierce hug. She stood back and gazed at him fondly. "You look wonderful, Sterne! As handsome as ever."

Sterne smiled. His sister loved him. She always had, even though he'd spent most of her life ignoring her and rebuffing her attempts to be close to him.

"You look pretty great yourself, Stace." He looked closely at her. What he'd said was true, he realized. He'd never seen her look prettier, or happier. Her thick nut-brown hair fell to her shoulders in soft waves, her tawny brown eyes were glowing, and her orange-and-yellow bathing suit displayed a lissome figure with no evidence of the pregnancy that had produced her twin daughters two years ago.

There was a shriek from the pool, and both Sterne and Stacey turned to see Amanda and Allison in hand-to-hand combat over a bright yellow rubber duck. Brynn calmly reached over and removed the duck from the water. The twins looked at her for a moment and then turned their attention to the other toys floating in the pool.

Sterne stared at Brynn. She didn't look at all like the skinny kid he'd insistently pictured in his mind during the drive here. Her bright auburn hair was piled on top of her head, exposing the gracefully alluring curve of her neck. She was wearing a sea-green maillot that emphasized her long, slim legs, the fullness of her breasts, and her slender waist. His gaze traveled over her compulsively. She was laughing at the babies' antics, and the beauty of her smile affected him deep in his groin. She removed her sunglasses and let one of the twins put them on, and he was stunned by the gorgeous pale green shade of her eyes. He remembered gazing into them as he held her in his arms, remembered the way her lips had parted for him when he lowered his mouth to hers . . .

Brynn was studiously ignoring Sterne. She concentrated her attention on Stacey's adorable twins and willed him away. She'd told Stacey nothing of what had happened between herself and Sterne. It was the first time she hadn't been able to confide in her friend.

Little Amanda handed her a vinyl mermaid doll and Brynn made the appropriately admiring noises. All the time she was excruciatingly aware of Sterne standing a few feet away, talking to Stacey. Her pulses were beginning to race. From the corner of her eye, she caught a glimpse of him.

Stacey was right—he looked as handsome as ever. He was tall and dark, and his royal blue polo shirt heightened the rich blue color of his eyes. His jeans fit all too well. Brynn was mesmerized by the way the faded denim hugged his muscular thighs and defined his . . . masculinity. Her throat was suddenly dry.

This was absurd, Sterne thought, stealing a look at Brynn. She hadn't even spoken to him! The family was sure to become suspicious if the two of them spent the entire weekend pointedly ignoring each other. He would be the one to take things in hand, he decided loftily. After all, Brynn Cassidy was nothing more than a longtime family friend.

"Hello, Brynn." He purposefully planted himself directly beside her chair.

She glanced up at him. "Hi." Her voice was casual, indifferent. She was quite proud of the way she'd pulled it off. No one would ever guess that her insides were quivering.

Sterne was totally taken aback. Brynn sounded completely uninterested, as if she'd spent the last week without giving him a thought, as if nothing had hap-

America's most popular, most compelling romance novels...

Here, at last...love stories that really involve you! Fresh, finely crafted novels with story lines so believable you'll feel you're actually living them! Characters you can relate to...exciting places to visit...unexpected plot twists...all in all, exciting romances that satisfy your mind and delight your heart.

Now you can be sure you'll never, ever miss a single Loveswept title by enrolling in our special reader's home delivery service. A service that will bring all four new Loveswept romances published every month into your home—and deliver them to you before they appear in the bookstores!

Examine 4 Loveswept Novels for

15 days FREE!

(SEE OTHER SIDE FOR DETAILS)

pened between them that had changed their relationship forever.

And then he knew how far he'd come. He didn't view Brynn as a longtime family friend. It was impossible to pretend that he did, even to himself. He saw her as a woman, one that he wanted with an intensity he'd never known. And he was supposed to spend the entire weekend pretending that he didn't.

Stacey didn't seem to find anything amiss. She was talking to Brynn, to the twins, oblivious of the tension between her brother and her best friend. And there *was* tension, Sterne insisted to himself. Sexual tension. Brynn was as aware of him as he was of her, he was sure of that. This damnable indifferent air she had directed toward him had to be an act.

He knelt beside her chair, casually placing one hand on the armrest. He had an unparalleled view of her bare thighs from this position. They were lightly tanned and looked silky smooth. They were firm and rounded and he imagined running his hands over the length of them, stroking them, opening them . . .

He cleared his throat. "So . . . uh, what have you been up to, Brynnie?"

She shrugged. "The usual."

"Seen anything of Daniel King?" He was determined to goad her, to knock her out of this uncharacteristic display of apathy.

Brynn clenched her jaw. Sterne, who claimed to have no memory for names, certainly hadn't had any trouble coming up with that one. "No, I haven't," she said tightly.

Stacey came in, right on cue, as Sterne had known she would. "Who's Daniel King, Brynnie?"

"Daniel King is a single woman's dream," Sterne replied before Brynn had a chance to speak. "He's a nice, normal, marriageable doctor . . . who dumped Brynn for a younger woman. I offered to make a play for the girl and give Brynn a chance to nab him on the rebound, but she—"

"Declined his generous offer," Byrnn finished for him.

"No wonder!" Stacey exclaimed, staring from one to the other. "Honestly, Sterne, no woman wants a man under those circumstances. It's downright insulting."

"Gee, I didn't mean to insult you, Brynnie," Sterne said with choirboy innocence, still kneeling beside her chair. "I just thought that when it came to landing a man, you needed all the help you could get."

It must have been fate that at that very moment, tiny Allison offered Brynn her red plastic pail filled with water. Brynn looked at Stacey. "Shall I?"

"By all means," said Stacey.

Brynn poured the water over Sterne's head. The twins chortled with laughter and began dumping water over their own heads in gleeful imitation. Stacey and Brynn laughed, too, as Sterne spluttered in wet protest.

"Oh, baby, you asked for it!" Sterne rose swiftly and grabbed Brynn's wrist, pulling her up from her chair. "You've had this coming for *years!*"

"Stacey! Help! Call off your brother!" Laughing, Brynn held out her other hand to Stacey.

Sterne caught that hand as well and jerked her toward him. "You have one minute to convince me why I shouldn't drown you in the ocean." He grinned down at her, his dark blue eyes teasing.

"Talk, Brynnie. Your time is running out." He tugged her closer, holding her hands against his chest. His knee slipped between her thighs.

"Sterne!" It was a strangled sound, somewhere between a laugh and a gasp. "Let me go!" He was too close. Her head was beginning to spin. He was the essence of masculinity and his sexual energy was commanding her senses.

"Let you go?" His laugh was low, and sexy. "You didn't even say please." He wrapped a powerful arm around her waist, molding her against his hard, burgeoning loins. "Say it, Brynnie. Say please."

She stared into his eyes, and saw the hot blue flames burning there. The laughter died in her throat. There didn't seem to be an inch of her body not touching him. Her breasts were nestled against his chest, her legs were hugging the muscular thigh he'd thrust between them, and her hips fit all too well against his unyielding male hardness. She felt breathless, hot, and aroused. Her insides were melting like sugar candy and she was aware of a warm, sweet liquid far down in the depths of her.

"Brynnie," Sterne murmured as he compulsively lowered his head to hers. Brynn's eyelids felt heavy. It was an effort to keep her eyes even partially open.

"Sterne, let Brynn go!" Stacey's sharp tones jarred them both from the sensual cocoon that had enveloped them. "Right now!"

Reluctantly, Sterne dropped his arms. Brynn took an awkward, stumbling step away from him. Both turned to face Stacey, who was staring at them while holding a twin perched on each hip. "What's going on with you two?" Stacey demanded, not smiling.

Sterne heaved his best imitation of a bored sigh. "We were just kidding around, Stace. Like we always do."

Stacey glowered at him. "You'd better do something about the look in your eye if you hope to convince anyone of that!"

"Same old Stacey." Sterne smiled an indulgent, brotherly smile. "Bossy, paranoid . . . Justin was a brave man to take you on." He walked away from them without a backward glance, heading to the house with a deliberate masculine swagger.

The twins wriggled in Stacey's arms and she set them down on the grass. "Brynnie, you and Sterne aren't . . . haven't . . ." Her voice trailed off. She was at a loss for words.

"There's nothing beween Sterne and me," Brynn hastened to assure her.

Stacey looked unconvinced. "Something's changed between you," she insisted. "I saw the way he was looking at you—and the way you were looking at him! If I hadn't been here, you would've—"

"He's kissed me a few times, Stacey, that's all." Brynn was aware that she was blushing. Since she'd been twelve years old, she'd been able to talk to Stacey about virtually anything . . . until now.

"Anyone who's spent as much time kissing as Sterne has must be fabulous at it," Stacey said worriedly. "Lord, Brynnie, I'd rather see you have your first affair with Muammar al-Qaddafi! You know what Sterne's like as well as I do. He'll hurt you—badly. Remember what Dr. Ruth said: 'a good lover is not necessarily a good man to love.' "

"I think it was Dear Abby who said that. Or was it Miss Manners?"

Stacey sighed with exasperation. "Whoever said it, the advice is valid. Sterne might have a charming facade when he chooses, but inside he . . . he's cold, Brynnie. He's unfeeling. He can't help but hurt anyone who cares about him because he cares about nobody but himself."

"I'd always thought that, too," Brynn said, staring into space, remembering, "but he's said some things that made me believe—"

"That underneath his rakish exterior is a lovable Boy Scout just waiting for the right woman to bring him out?" Stacey rolled her eyes. "Ah, Brynnie, come on! You *can't* have fallen for that one!" She slipped her arm around Brynn's waist and gave her an affectionate squeeze. "Brynn, you're my dearest friend. I love you more than I would've loved any sister. I've always been closer to you than to anyone in my family, and I just can't stand the thought of Sterne hurting you. Please, please, think with your head and not with your hormones!"

It was the same advice she would have given a friend who found herself attracted to Sterne Lipton, Brynn silently acknowledged. She gazed into her closest friend's worried brown eyes. "Don't worry about me, Stace. My common sense has been ruling my hormones for

years. And I'm not going to have an affair with Sterne—
or with Muammar al-Qaddafi."

They smiled at each other in mutual understanding,
then each scooped up a twin and went inside the airy,
sprawling house.

Later that evening Fred Rhodes, the president's aide-
de-camp, announced to the family that Bradford Lipton's arrival would be delayed until the following day,
due to pressing congressional business.

"Mrs. Lipton has delayed her departure from Washington as well," Rhodes said stiffly, glancing warily at
the roomful of assorted Liptons. "I've come to . . . er,
make preparations for the President's arrival tomorrow."

"What's to prepare?" Sterne drawled laconically. "The
household staff takes care of everything here. There's
nothing for you to do but to run interference between
us and the press. That's why you're really here, isn't it,
Freddie? To keep us from creating some sort of incident that might embarrass the prez."

Fred Rhodes began to perspire. "It does seem that
every time all of you are together, something manages
to occur which . . . er . . . er—"

"Places the President in an awkward position," Justin Marks finished for him. "You've got your work cut
out for you, Rhodes."

Stacey slipped her hand into her husband's. "Remember when it used to be you who tried to keep a lid
on the Liptons, Justin?"

Justin nodded, grinning. "I decided if you can't lick
'em, join 'em."

"Relax, Fred," Spence Lipton said gently. "It's going
to be a tranquil weekend. Neptune's fifth moon is in
alignment to—"

"Please!" Rhodes interrupted a little desperately. "No
astrology. No tarot cards. No tea-leaf reading."

"There are undercurrents." Spence's long-haired wife
Patty spoke up from the corner where she was nursing

her eight-month-old daughter. The couple's older children, Sunshine, Melody, and Aurora, aged six, five, and four, had already been tucked into bed along with Stacey and Justin's twins. "The vibrations are very strong. We didn't take into account the effect of Halley's Comet when we charted, Spence. Changes are coming. It's all around us." She smiled serenely. Patty was always serene. "Freddie, would you like me to brew you a cup of camomile tea?"

"Vibes and changes, comets and camomile tea," Sterne murmured to Brynn. He'd flopped down beside her on the wide chaise longue on the far side of the screened porch. She'd been as surprised as the rest of the Liptons when Sterne had elected to spend the evening at home rather than join the weekend singles' revelry at Sterne's Place Two. "Maybe old Freddie had better pour himself a triple Scotch." He grinned at Brynn.

She smiled back, and for a moment there was no one in the room but the two of them, sharing a private joke. Sterne looked remarkably respectable in khaki slacks and a yellow polo shirt. She crossed her legs and smoothed the skirt of her lavender knit sundress, suddenly aware of just how close he was sitting to her. Their shoulders and thighs were touching.

She glanced across the room and found Stacey and Justin watching her, their expressions speculative. Self-consciously, Brynn leaned away from Sterne as color rose in her cheeks.

Lucas, the six-foot-four, two-hundred-and-sixty-five pound "baby" of the Lipton family, cleared his throat. "Actually, there's something I wanted to tell Dad and Mom."

The defensive linebacker for the University of Nebraska stared at his shoes, looking downright anxious. "I want to drop out of school," he said. "I'm tired of playing football and I'm tired of trying to pass courses that I don't understand. I'm going to quit."

"Quit college?" Fred Rhodes echoed in a squeak. He had actually paled at the announcement. "Lucas, you

can't quit! You only have one more year till you gradu-
ate. You're a starter on the football team. And you're
sure to be drafted next spring by the pros, possibly as
high as the second round, according to our sources."

"And the voters like the idea of the President's son
playing football," Spence added caustically. "Having Lucas drop out is a potential political liability." He crossed
the room and shook his younger brother's hand. "I'm
behind you all the way, Lucas. Patty and I want you to
know you're always welcome at the farm. If you're looking for answers, I think you'll find them when you're
close to nature. Your soul expands when . . ."

"Look at Freddie's face," Sterne whispered in an aside
to Brynn as Spence expounded on his personal theory
of universal oneness. "It's an awesome shade of purple."

"He knows that he's going to be taking the heat for
Lucas's decision." Brynn glanced at Rhodes, who was
practically wringing his hands in despair. "Your father
isn't going to be pleased."

"And of course, Dad won't deal with Lucas directly,"
Sterne said thoughtfully. "I wonder if Lucas would
change his mind if he did? Do you suppose this is all a
bid for Dad's attention?"

"Probably," she said. She'd spent years watching
various Lipton offspring vie for their father's attention.
They never got it. Bradford Lipton expressed his dis-
pleasure to his aides and left them to handle his recal-
citrant family.

"Do you suppose that's why I've done some of the
things I've done?" Sterne asked slowly. He looked thunderstruck, as if he'd accidentally stumbled onto one of
life's great truths. "To get my father's attention?"

Brynn suppressed a smile. It didn't require much
insight to recognize the motivation behind Sterne's
outrageous behavior. She'd guessed at it years ago.
And he hadn't? Well, he'd always claimed he wasn't
introspective. How strange that he'd actually had an
insightful moment after all these years.

"But it's so stupid," he murmured, staring into

Brynn's eyes. "My father's political career is the most important thing in his life. It always has been and it always will be. I could play the rebel till I'm ninety-two and it wouldn't change my father's priorities. Or even affect him. Only my own life is . . . affected."

"Spence and Stacey realized that ages ago," Brynn said softly. "They're happy living their own lives, away from the shadow of Bradford Lipton. They have families of their own, and can get from them what they missed. They can give to them what they wanted to give and couldn't."

"Love," Sterne said in another astonishing flash of insight. "That's what you mean, isn't it, Brynnie?"

"Well, yes. But I didn't want to be accused of sounding like a mawkishly sentimental card."

He stood up. "I need some air. Come for a walk with me, Brynnie." He gripped her elbow and tugged her to her feet.

They were on the beach now. The sky and water merged into an endless expanse of blackness, punctuated only by the crescent moon and stars and an occasional whitecap. It was dark and quiet and private. Brynn's gaze flickered from Sterne to the lights of the house.

"Don't look so wary," he said lightly. "I asked you to go for a walk. I'm not going to pounce . . . unless you want me to?"

Unfortunately, she did, Brynn admitted achingly to herself. The deserted beach seemed incredibly romantic and she'd spent a whole week yearning for his touch. Her blood hummed with an explosive combination of sensuality and expectation. "No, I . . ." she began slowly, but it was too late. She had waited too long with her denial, giving herself away.

"So you do want me," he said as he carefully, slowly— as if he had all the time in the world—drew her into his arms. Their gazes met and held.

"I shouldn't," she whispered, even as she slipped her arms around his neck. "Your own sister warned me against you. She said you'll hurt me and I know she's right and yet . . . and yet . . ." She gazed into his warm, dark blue eyes.

"And yet?" he prompted, brushing her lips with his. "Say it, sweetheart. Tell me that you want me."

She was surprised at the plea in his voice, as if he were uncertain, as if he really did need to hear her say those words. But that was impossible, of course. Sterne Lipton knew she wanted him. He knew women the way doctoral candidates know their own dissertations, inside and out.

She swallowed and said nothing. He arched her body into his, one hand locking her against him while the other caressed her back. "Why did you run out on me last week, Brynnie?" he asked softly. His hand traced the line of her ribs beneath the soft cotton. His thumb brushed over her nipple, which was taut and straining against the material of her dress.

"I spent a whole week thinking about you, wanting you," he murmured against her ear, his voice deep and low. His hand continued its journey, stroking her shoulder, following the line of her collarbone, pausing to smooth her throat before proceeding with heartstopping inevitability down the scoop neckline of her dress.

Brynn stood still, her arms linked loosely around his neck, shivering with the searing pleasure his slow, light caresses were giving her. She drew in her breath when his hand slipped beneath the cotton dress and he cupped her bare breast in his palm.

She thought she should protest, but the only sound she made was a soft moan as his finger circled her nipple. She closed her eyes and arched closer, her breathing quickening.

She felt a shudder of desire go through him and was inflamed by the sensuous movements of his hips. He wanted her as much as she wanted him, and the realization thrilled her. "Sterne," she whispered as she brushed her lips along the strong line of his jaw. "I—I missed you this week too."

Her soft words affected him as deeply as a physical caress. *She'd missed him.* Sterne knew in that moment that his feelings this past week had involved more than merely thinking of her, more than wanting her in his bed. He'd been missing her.

The idea was so novel that Sterne was jolted out of the all-consuming wildness of his passion. He'd never missed anyone in his life, at least not since his mother had died. He'd protected himself so well from the pain of missing anyone that he hadn't even recognized what he'd been feeling until now, when Brynn had told him.

He felt so strange. He wished someone would explain what he was going through now. He didn't understand this surge of emotion, an inexplicable mixture of tenderness and passion. He wanted to be gentle with Brynn at the same time that he wanted to lower her to the sand and crush her body against his. He wanted to protect her and to ravish her at the same time.

She was deeply aroused. He knew by the way she was clinging to him, moving against him. She was hot for him! he thought exultantly. Her mouth claimed his and she parted her lips, inviting him to sample the sweetness within. Her tongue darted into his mouth and rubbed his tongue as she ran her slender hands over him, caressing him. Sterne groaned with pleasure. He was sure if he were to suggest that they walk down the beach to his condo, she would acquiesce.

They could be alone there, completely alone, and he would lay her down on the thick cushions of the long, wide white sofa and . . . Even as he tantalized himself with such erotic images, Sterne slowly removed his hand from her breast and cupped her shoulders to gently put her away from him.

He simply couldn't bring himself to try to rush Brynn into bed. She deserved more than that. He was going to have her, he promised himself as his body ached and throbbed with unsatisfied arousal. But not until the time was right. He wondered briefly how and when he would know when that was. Putting someone else's needs ahead of his own was entirely new to him.

Brynn was smiling at him, and she stroked his cheek with her hand. "I have a strong feeling that the others are going to join us at any minute," she said softly, her eyes warm.

"To rescue sweet little Brynnie from the big, bad wolf?" He caught her hand and pressed his lips to her palm.

She grinned. "Something like that."

"And you didn't want to be rescued at all." He could see it in her eyes, and the revelation delighted him. As he stared down at her, he suddenly felt dizzy and dazed and lost in the green glow of her gaze. "Brynnie, would you have come to my apartment with me tonight?" he heard himself ask in a voice he scarcely recognized as his own.

She took both his hands in hers and her smile dazzled him. Her eyes shone in the moonlight. "Of course not, Sterne," she said in melting tones.

Seven

Her reply floored him. "What do you mean, of course not?" Sterne demanded.

Brynn laughed up at him. "You figure it out. It shouldn't be too hard for one who claims to have such a high IQ."

"Let's leave my IQ out of this." He fastened his hands around her waist. Vaguely, he thought he ought to be angry with her, but he couldn't for the life of him summon even an ounce of rage. Another amazing first for Sterne Lipton. His masculine pride had definitely taken a hit, and his only reaction was mild amusement.

"I thought I'd made the ultimate sacrifice for you tonight," he said, "by stopping and not hustling you off to bed when you seemed to be weakening. Are you telling me that my noble gesture was all in vain? That you weren't weakening at all, and you would've stopped me yourself?"

She stared at him. "You made a noble gesture on my behalf?"

"And you didn't even notice." He smiled dryly. "I

suppose that's why I felt the need to point it out to you. Acts of unselfishness don't exactly come naturally to me."

How well she knew! Impulsively, she threw her arms around him and hugged him tight. "Thank you for making one for me, Sterne," she whispered.

His arms came up to enfold her. For a moment they stood in silence, holding each other close. Then Sterne buried his lips in the scented hollow of her throat. "I like this," he murmured huskily. "I think I could get used to—"

"Someone's coming!" she interrupted in a whisper. Still clasped in his embrace, she turned her head to the wooden stairs leading from the Lipton house to the beach. "It's Patty with little China Star."

Sterne followed Brynn's gaze to see his sister-in-law floating serenely down the steps, holding her baby in her arms. By unspoken mutual consent, Brynn and Sterne moved out of each other's arms.

"Oh, there you are!" Patty said as she and her baby joined them. They were followed seconds later by Spence, Lucas, Stacey, and Justin.

"Yeah, here we are," Sterne said, casting a conspiratorial glance at Brynn. "All of you suddenly got the urge for a little fresh air, too, eh?"

"We wanted to get away from Fred," Lucas said. "I think he's lost it this time. He's pacing around mumbling about *Monday Night Football* and voting viewers."

"Well, I just want you to know that I'm behind you one hundred percent, Lucas," Sterne said heartily, putting a brotherly arm around the younger man's shoulders. "And if you need a place to stay, you're welcome to move in with me."

Lucas stared at him in amazement. "You mean it, Sterne?"

Sterne shrugged. Everybody's eyes were upon him. "Sure, kid."

"But you always said that having someone live with

you would cramp your style," Lucas said in confusion. "Won't I cramp your style?"

"Hell, yes," replied Sterne. "But you're welcome to move in, anyway."

Brynn smiled at him. "That's very generous of you to offer, Sterne."

"It's unbelievable of him to offer," an incredulous Stacey added.

"Lucas appreciates the offer," Spence said, "but he's coming to Fredericksburg and staying with Patty and the kids and me at the farm."

"It's in the stars," Patty said dreamily.

Lucas stared up at the night sky with obvious bewilderment.

Sterne and Brynn caught each other's eye and grinned. Stacey insisted they go for a walk on the beach, and as all the Liptons walked together in the sand, it seemed perfectly natural for Brynn to slip her hand into Sterne's.

No one was too surprised when Fred Rhodes received a telephone call the next morning informing him that Bradford Lipton would be unable to make it to Rehoboth Beach after all. One of the congressional party leaders was holding a picnic in his home district and had asked the President to put in an appearance. Bradford Lipton was renowned for his party loyalty. Caroline Lipton's regrets were conveyed to the younger Liptons via Fred Rhodes, as well as her invitation for the family to remain at the beach house for as long as they wished.

Sterne's mind was far away from the senior Liptons' absence. He was staring across the breakfast table at Brynn. Lord, she looked good in the morning, he thought. She was wearing some sort of flowered caftan and her hair fell around her shoulders in incredibly appealing disarray. He wondered if she was naked under the robe, and a flash of electricity seemed to jolt through him at the image that thought evoked.

A sleepy-eyed Brynn desultorily sipped her coffee as

the conversation swirled around her. She had lain awake for a long time last night, thinking about Sterne—of course—and reliving every moment she had spent in his arms. Last night on the beach was as close as she'd ever come to surrendering to him. Sterne was right, she was weakening.

She glanced up and found him watching her. He wasn't even pretending to listen to the breakfast table conversation, but was staring at her, his dark blue eyes intense. She met and held his gaze. Everything and everyone else was relegated to a background haze as the two of them focused only on each other.

"Since the folks aren't coming, will you be going back to D.C. today, Sterne?" Stacey asked pointedly, deliberately breaking the bond of unspoken communication between her brother and her closest friend. "I mean, it's Saturday night, your night to howl and prowl and—and whatever else you do."

"He can do all the howling and prowling and whatever else right here in Rehoboth Beach," Lucas said with a chortle. "At Sterne's Place Two. That's where I'm heading tonight."

"Sterne no longer howls and prowls," Patty said, smiling benignly as she shoveled mushy rice cereal into her baby's mouth. "He's moving into quieter pursuits."

Stacey stared at her. "How do you know that, Patty?"

"She read it in the stars," Sterne said caustically. He rose abruptly and pushed back his chair. Patty spooked him. He'd seen the knowing look in her eyes as she glanced from Brynn to himself. No longer howls and prowls, she'd said. As if he were an alley cat who'd been tamed. Or . . . a former swinging bachelor who'd settled down with one woman. The notion was enough to make his hair stand on end.

"I'm going for a swim," he announced, and quickly departed.

Spence entered the kitchen accompanied by his three little girls. "Uncle Sterne almost knocked me over," grumbled six-year-old Sunshine.

"He went by like a streak of lightning," Spence said. "Why is he in such an all-fired hurry this morning?"

"He's running from fate," Patty said, smiling at Brynn.

"You can't run from fate," Spence argued.

Brynn blushed. "If you'll all excuse me, I think I'll get dressed and . . . uh, head into town to do a little shopping."

Spence and Patty exchanged glances. "You can't run from fate," they chorused.

Though warned they couldn't run from fate, Brynn and Sterne did an excellent job of avoiding each other for the remainder of the day. He swam in the pool while she spent the afternoon at the beach, building sand castles with the little girls and swimming in the surf. At dinnertime Sterne took off to eat in town, and Brynn joined the rest of the Liptons for a barbeque on the lawn.

Saturday night loomed. All six children were bathed and put to bed, Spence and Patty took out their Ouija board for consultation, and Justin and Stacey eyed each other like a pair of besotted newlyweds. There was no sign of Sterne.

"Hey, Brynnie, I'm going out to howl and prowl," Lucas said jovially, splashing an alarming amount of lime-scented cologne on his neck. "Care to come along?"

Brynn weighed her other options: feeling increasingly *de trop* with an amorous Stacey and Justin, or chatting up the spirits with Spence and Patty. Did she really have a choice? She linked her arm through Lucas's. "Let's howl and prowl, Lucas." She hoped she sounded more enthusiastic than she felt.

She was getting too old for this, Brynn thought four and a half hours later as she nursed a soda in yet another bar. She'd sat through a wet T-shirt contest, a teeny-weeny-bikini contest, a manliest-chest contest (Lucas had been a participant in that one and hadn't won, much to his outrage), and a wet-nightgown contest.

She'd endured rounds of risqué songs sung by tipsy fraternity boys, and declined numerous beer-chugging challenges.

Lucas was clearly having the time of his life, but Brynn was not. It was a lot like baby-sitting without getting paid, she decided, as she dragged Lucas away from an altercation that threatened to explode into a good old-fashioned brawl.

"Time to go home, Lucas," she told him with forced cheeriness. Her fingers were hooked into his belt and she pulled him along after her. Fortunately, Lucas seemed willing to let her lead the way. He'd been accustomed to having her drag him around since he was a little boy, and the fact that he was now almost three times her size seemed to have escaped his notice.

"We haven't gone to Sterne's bar yet," Lucas said as she stuffed him into the passenger seat of his car, a bright red Corvette. Unlike his older brother, Lucas was perfectly amenable to having her drive his car.

"We're not going there tonight, Lucas. It's . . . uh, closed."

"Closed?" Lucas stared at his watch. After some deliberation, he came up with the time. "It doesn't close till three in the morning," he said emphatically. "We can still make it."

"I'm not going there, Lucas."

"Why not?"

"Because I'm sick and tired of seeing your brother in the company of a never-ending supply of blonde bimbos and brunette bimbos and redhaired bimbos—"

"And no-haired bimbos," put in Lucas. "Remember that freaky girl who shaved her head?"

Brynn clenched her teeth. "Yes." Thank heavens Lucas wasn't at all perceptive. She had just confessed to the jealousy that burned through her at the thought of Sterne with other women. "I want to go home now, Lucas."

"Okay." He sighed, then immediately brightened. "We

had a blast tonight, didn't we, Brynnie? You can howl and prowl with me anytime."

Not on your life, Brynn told him silently. But she managed to smile. "Thanks, Lucas."

"Where in the hell have you been?" Sterne asked harshly, giving her a slight shake. And then he inhaled. "You smell like a brewery! Are you drunk?"

"Shh, quiet now," Lucas admonished, duplicating Brynn's exact tone and inflection. "We don't want to wake anybody." From anyone else, it would have been sarcasm. Lucas, however, was dutifully passing on Brynn's orders.

"I'm not drunk," Brynn said coolly.

"No, Brynnie stuck to diet soda all night," Lucas said. "She smells like beer because some guy spilled it on her," he continued blithely. "He was such a fun guy, huh, Brynnie? What was his name?"

"Eddie the Octopus." Brynn recalled the high-spirited college junior with a grimace. "He was a fun guy, all right."

Sterne shot Lucas a scathing glance before turning to Brynn, his blue eyes flashing. "You've been missing for nearly five hours!"

"Missing?" She stared at him uncomprehendingly. "We weren't missing. Lucas's Secret Service agents were with us the entire time." And from their glum expressions during the evening, the agents had found the adolescent high jinks and ribaldry as tedious as she had, Brynn thought.

"No!" Sterne shook his head. "I asked Rivington and his partner to contact Lucas's agents and he said that he couldn't, that you and Lucas had given them the slip."

"They probably wished we had, but we didn't. Those two poor agents were right with us every step of the way."

"Why would Rivington lie?" Sterne demanded. "He

knew I was going out of my mind, wondering where in the hell you were, wondering if you were safe or—or—" He paused, remembering his frantic tirade to Agent Rivington. "Or had met another man."

A thoroughly infuriating idea struck him. "That's why Rivington lied!" He glared at Brynn. "You were in cahoots with him, weren't you? You both wanted me to think that you'd picked up some other guy. You deliberately plotted the whole thing to—to make me jealous!"

Brynn shook her head in disbelief. "Get real, Sterne," she said lightly. "If I wanted to make you jealous, I would've found a way that didn't include trailing after Lucas to one adolescent watering hole after another."

"Tonight was totally out of hand, wasn't it, Brynnie?" Lucas said rhapsodically. "You should've been along, Sterne. We hit the coolest places in town." He named the bars to which they'd gone.

Sterne was aghast. "You don't take a woman like Brynn to those—those zoos, you moron!" he snapped, turning his anger on Lucas.

Lucas looked confused. "But we had fun, didn't we, Brynnie?"

Brynn smiled fondly at him. Lucas would always be her exuberant and slightly befuddled surrogate kid brother. "Fun doesn't come close to describing it, Lucas. I only hope that the photographer who took all those pictures of you in the manliest-chest contest doesn't decide to sell them to the tabloids." She turned to Sterne. "All the contestants had to strip to their shorts and parade along a makeshift runway. Lucas really threw himself into the role."

Lucas beamed. "Yeah, it was great. Remember that blonde fox who stuck her phone number in my jockey shorts, Brynnie? Hey, is it still there?" He began to unzip his trousers to check.

"Wait!" Sterne caught his arm, halting him. "I think it's time you went to bed, little brother." He began to haul Lucas from the room, pausing to look over his shoulder at Brynn. "I'll talk to *you* later, lady."

"No, you won't." Brynn wrinkled her nose as she sniffed the pungent aroma of beer emanating from her blouse and slacks. She really *did* smell like a brewery. "I'm going to take a shower and go to bed. Good night, Lucas," she called to her escort of the evening.

Brynn showered and shampooed her hair, then towel-dried and combed it. She wrapped a thick green bath towel around herself and padded into the rose and beige bedroom that she always used during her visits.

"Such a modest little virgin. Keeps properly covered, even when she thinks she's alone in her room."

The sound of the mocking masculine voice stopped her cold in her tracks. Brynn gaped at the figure reclining on her bed. Sterne, clad in an old pair of cutoffs, lay propped against the pillows, his legs crossed casually at the ankles. His eyes were gleaming as he flashed that bad-boy smile of his.

Brynn drew in a sharp breath and continued to stare. She'd imagined him this way so many times that, for one wild moment, she thought perhaps she was hallucinating.

"What are you doing here?" she asked breathlessly. Her gaze traveled over him, compulsively following the length of his hard, muscular frame. No, the man lying on her bed, devouring her with hungry blue eyes, was no apparition.

He sat up. "I told you I'd talk to you later." He was grinning at her, thoroughly enjoying her discomfiture. "And you told me you were going to take a shower and go to bed. I took that as an invitation to join you. Sorry I missed the shower. Lucas needed a lot of help getting into bed. He's half-witted when he's sober, so when he's drunk he has no wits at all. But I'm here now. Ready to go to bed?"

Brynn walked over to the bedroom door and opened it. "Good night, Sterne," she said calmly. She didn't feel calm and she wished she were wearing something a little more formidable than a towel. But she knew that as long as Sterne got a rise out of her, his teasing would escalate. Her only recourse was to play it cool.

He rose slowly and ambled to the door, stopping directly in front of her. "You don't really want me to go, Brynnie." His voice was soft, low, mesmerizingly seductive.

Brynn steeled herself against it. "Yes, I do. I have to radio Rivington and plot out the next move in our game plan."

"Okay, okay!" Sterne's expression was a mixture of irritation and amusement. "I was way out of line to accuse you of plotting with Rivington. I apologize. Obviously, Rivington decided to teach me a lesson or something all on his own. I've always known the guy doesn't approve of me. And you went with Lucas tonight to keep him out of trouble."

"And because Stacey and Justin wanted to go to bed early and Spence and Patty wanted to conjure up their spiritual guides from some other plane. I didn't feel like retiring to my room with a book, so I went out with Lucas. Agent Rivington was *not* consulted."

Sterne took a step closer. "Would you have gone out with me tonight, Brynn?"

"We'll never know, will we?" she snapped. "You weren't here to ask me."

"You're jealous, aren't you, honey?" His face lit with a smile of pure masculine triumph. "Did you think I was with another woman?"

Their gazes clashed. Stormy pale green eyes and intent deep blue ones. Brynn was the first to look away. She stared down at the rose carpet. "Yes, dammit," she whispered fiercely. "Yes, to both questions. Now get out of my room."

"Maybe you ought to talk to Rivington." Sterne cupped her jaw and tilted her head up. His eyes trapped hers. "He could tell you exactly how I spent the evening. I went to the bar and had a cheeseburger for dinner, then I worked on the books for an hour or so. I drove around town for a while. Alone. I was alone the whole time. I came back here at nine-thirty."

She swallowed. "Lucas and I left here at nine-fifteen."

"I came back determined to play it straight with you. I'd spent the whole day missing you like crazy and I decided it was time to stop kidding myself and playing stupid games. I want you, Brynn. More than I've ever wanted any woman." His voice faltered. "And it—what I feel for you—goes beyond sexual wanting." He expelled his breath in a rush and lowered his eyes. His cheeks were slightly flushed.

Tenderness surged through Brynn, and she leaned forward, linking her arms around his neck. "You sound as if you've been rehearsing that," she said softly, rubbing her nose against his.

"I have," he admitted somewhat sheepishly. "For hours. All day while I was in self-exile in the pool, wanting to be with you at the beach. During dinner when I wished we were together in some romantic candlelit restaurant. And all night, while I paced the floor and worried that you'd meet some guy who would sweep you off your feet and I'd never have the chance to . . ." His voice trailed off.

"Never have the chance to what, Sterne?" she whispered, nuzzling the hard, tanned column of his neck.

His arms encircled her and pulled her close. "To make love to you. To tell you how I feel about you." He heaved a shuddering groan. "I'm crazy about you, Brynnie. I don't know how it happened, but I can't seem to stop thinking about you, missing you when you're not with me, wanting you. . . ."

Her heart surged with joy. She'd known Sterne long enough to realize that such an admission was totally foreign to him. Sterne Lipton could spin a spellbinding line when he chose, but it always involved lavish compliments for his intended conquest, never a declaration of his own feelings.

She drew back a little and gazed up at him, and in that moment she knew she was in love with him. She'd been fighting the realization, fighting herself, fighting him . . . all in vain. She didn't know how or when it had happened, but there it was. She loved him.

Did he read it in her eyes? she wondered. Or did he interpret the radiant glow he saw there as her imminent sexual surrender?

"Let me stay with you tonight, Brynnie," he murmured hoarsely, holding her tight against him. "Don't send me away, sweetheart."

She clung to him. She couldn't send him away, not even if she wanted to. Her own need had been heightened by the realization of her love for him. She felt as if she was burning hot and freezing cold, all at the same time. She felt as if she were standing at the end of a high-dive and had to decide whether to jump off or to retreat to the safety of familiar ground.

She took a deep breath. She couldn't withdraw. She couldn't send Sterne away. She was a woman who longed to give herself to the man she loved. Her heart pounding, she dared to run her hands over the whipcord muscles of his arms. Her fingers strayed to his bare chest and she toyed timidly with the wiry dark hair that covered it. "I—I don't want you to leave, Sterne. Stay with me."

"Oh, Brynnie," he breathed. He slowly, quietly closed the bedroom door and locked it. Then his fingers loosened the edges of her towel. It fell to the floor, and she stood naked and trembling before him.

Brynn had never felt so vulnerable, but she wasn't frightened. She was excited and curious and intrigued. And she was in love with the man who was gazing at her with such passion.

"You're beautiful," he said huskily, running his hands over the curves of her body. He gave a low, deep laugh. "Do you know how many times I pictured you like this? But my imagination didn't do you justice." His hands cupped her breasts. "So white and soft. And so firm. That should be a contradiction in terms." He began to knead lightly, erotically, with his fingers. "But it's not. It's not at all."

Brynn drew in a shaky, shuddery breath. She seemed to have lost the ability to think or move or even speak. She could only stand before him, listening to his husky voice while his big hands caressed her with a possessive ardor that made her head spin.

"And I didn't know your nipples would be so pink." His thumbs flicked over them, then circled them. She felt as if invisible wires carried hot currents straight to her most secret places. She throbbed and squirmed and emitted a breathless little moan.

"So hard and tight." His fingers continued their sensual play. "Do you like it when I touch you this way, my Brynnie?"

She managed to nod her head. Desire was flooding her, and her body was overwhelmed by the rush of thrilling new sensations his clever fingers were evoking. His hand moved lower, to the slender hollow of her waist, over the flatness of her stomach and the smooth curve of her hip. His fingers tangled in the thatch of downy curls. "You're blushing, Brynnie."

She slowly raised her eyes to his. "I—I was waiting for you to make some wisecrack about my being a natural redhead."

"No wisecracks tonight, sweetheart," he said tenderly. He smiled at her, then took her into his embrace and kissed the top of her head.

"How can you resist?" she murmured, holding onto him tightly. "There's an entire repertory of jokes about nervous virgins."

He scooped her up in his arms with one easy movement. "Are you a nervous virgin, Brynnie?"

She moistened her lips with the tip of her tongue. "A little, I guess."

He carried her to the bed and laid her down on it, then stretched out beside her, propping himself up on one elbow. "Only a little?"

"A lot," she confessed with a tremulous smile. "It must seem stupid to a veteran like you."

Her anxious little smile went straight to his heart. He tried to remember his first time. Lord, it seemed like ages ago! He'd been so young and reckless and had thrived on the forbidden danger of it all. What would it be like to face it as an adult, complete with an adult's caution and self-doubt? He could hardly fathom it, but he tried.

It was all new to him, this placing himself in another's skin and experiencing her feelings. He wanted to ease Brynn's insecurity, but how? The disparity in their sexual experience seemed too glaring merely to brush aside. Then he thought of a way.

He stared deeply into Brynn's eyes. "It's kind of a first for me too," he said softly, tracing his finger along the length of her collarbone. "I've never made love to a virgin before. I never wanted that kind of responsibility." He'd never wanted *any* responsibility for anyone or anything, he admitted to himself. But now . . . He bent to brush his lips along the path his fingers had followed.

"Don't be afraid, Brynnie." He curved his hand around the nape of her neck and began a slow massage. "There's nothing to worry about. I'll take care of you. I *want* to take care of you. It's going to be good, sweetheart. I promise to make it good for you." His voice was low and soothing. "Just relax, darling. Relax and let me make love to you."

He kissed her the way he'd been wanting to kiss her for hours, days, weeks. Deep and hot and hungry. Demanding. Possessive. He caressed her breasts while he kissed her, gently rubbing her taut, sensitized nipples until Brynn felt limp and liquid with desire.

When he lifted his mouth from hers she made a small, whimpering sound of protest, and he laughed huskily. "It's all right, love, I'm not going anywhere." He trailed a string of stinging kisses along the slender curve of her neck, his mouth moving ever lower. When his lips caught one aching, engorged nipple between them, Brynn gasped and clenched her hands into tight fists.

The sensations coursing through her were electric and wild, unlike anything she'd ever experienced. Sterne continued to pleasure her nipples with his lips and his tongue and his teeth while his hands fondled and stroked. She clutched his head to her breasts, her breath rasping in her throat.

"Please," she whispered, tossing her head back and forth against the pillow. It was so new, so intense. She was out of her head, out of control; she was exhilarated and a little scared at the same time. Her common sense had been replaced by powerful sensual forces that seemed to be commanded entirely by Sterne. This hot, honeyed sense of helplessness threatened to overpower her, she realized with a flash of alarm.

"Sterne . . ." Her voice sounded weak and uncertain to her own ears.

Sterne heard all the weakness and uncertainty in her protest and was tempted to ignore her feelings. He could sense her body beginning to stiffen in resistance, and he was tempted to ignore that too. It would be easy for him to overwhelm her and sweep her into an impassioned, unthinking surrender. She was clearly no match for a man of his sexual experience. He was on the verge of doing exactly that. After all, Sterne Lipton never put anyone or anything ahead of his own immediate gratification.

Instead, he sat up and pulled Brynn up alongside him, tucking her into the curve of his body. He was astonished to realize that he didn't want to overwhelm her with his sexual prowess, that he didn't want her unthinking surrender. He wanted her to be a willing partner, to give herself freely to him. He was momentarily struck dumb by the realization—and its corollary: if his own gratification had to be postponed, so be it.

"Sterne?" Brynn murmured softly.

"What's the matter, honey?" he heard himself ask, in incredibly patient tones.

She gulped. "I don't know. I . . . started to feel as if I were—were sinking in quicksand or something." She flushed. "I know it's a stupid analogy, but . . ."

"It's all right, sweetheart." He kissed her temple. "Probably just a touch of the famed virginal panic we've all been hearing about for the past twenty centuries." He knew now exactly why he'd avoided virgins like the plague. Smooth operators were not renowned for their patience or understanding in passionate sexual situations. And he certainly qualified as a world-class smooth operator. From where was he drawing this totally uncharacteristic patience and understanding? he mused.

"You have every right to be angry with me," she said. "I feel like an idiot."

He could feel her beginning to relax. He continued to hold her and stroke her, and kept his voice quiet and kind.

"Do I seem angry?" he asked.

"No." She gazed up at him trustingly. Sterne felt as if he'd been kicked in the stomach. When she looked at him that way, he knew he would manage to give her whatever she needed from him. Whatever, whenever, even if it ran contrary to his own desires of the moment. It was a profound and deeply affecting revelation.

There was a long moment of silence, and suddenly, Brynn giggled. " 'A touch of the famed virginal panic we've all been hearing about for the past twenty centuries'?" she repeated incredulously.

Sterne stared at her. The doubt and anxiety that had clouded her face had disappeared entirely. She was grinning at him, her eyes bright with laughter. And her hands were making provocative forays along his chest.

"You make it sound like a clinical condition," she said, "complete with recognizable symptoms, like malaria."

He raised his brows. "Would I be wrong in assuming that your symptoms have disappeared? Dare I believe that I've effected a cure?"

She snuggled closer, her fingertips tracing his navel with studied deliberation. "I guess I needed to talk about what was happening to me, Sterne. Thank you for being so nice to me."

He caught her hand and carried it to his mouth. "Do you want me to leave?" He held his breath as he awaited her answer, for he knew beyond a shadow of a doubt that he would abide by it. Sterne Lipton, that avid, salacious rake, would allow himself to be sent on his way, without trying to change her mind.

Brynn rolled on top of him. The wiry hair on his chest tickled her breasts and the rough denim of his cutoffs against her own bare limbs reminded her that he was still partially clad. She leaned down to brush her lips against his mouth. "No, I don't want you to leave," she whispered huskily.

His hands slowly stroked the length of her spine. "Do you want to make love, Brynnie?"

Her eyelids drifted closed and her mouth opened over his. "Oh, yes, Sterne," she breathed, just before their lips met in a deep, soul-shattering kiss.

Eight

Within moments, Brynn was catapulted back into the mindless, sensual pleasure that previously had engulfed her. But this time it didn't alarm her. Sterne had been so kind, so understanding of her foolish attack of nerves. She trusted him. Whatever happened in this room, this bed, tonight, she would be safe with Sterne, she thought warmly. She loved him, and after his uncharacteristic response to her virginal inhibitions, she knew that he cared for her too.

He could have scorned her, he could have forced her . . . but he'd done neither of those things. She kissed him with all the love and passion she'd kept locked inside her all these years. She gave it freely to him, loving him, needing him, wanting to belong to him with a primal feminine urgency.

Sterne skimmed his hands along her thighs, and he remembered how much he had wanted to touch her like this when he'd seen her in her bathing suit yesterday. Her skin was just as silky smooth as it looked, just as supple.

She flexed her knee and he stroked her inner thighs, tracing exciting, erotic little patterns on the exquisitely soft skin there. His fingers slipped between her legs and found her sweetly swollen. She gasped at the intimacy of his touch.

"So hot and wet," he whispered against her mouth. "And all for me." He felt possessive and protective.

"Yes," she murmured, clinging to him. He was so hard and strong and male. She loved the complementary differences between them. His masculinity heightened and enhanced her femininity. What was happening between them was magical and mysterious, a rapturous combination of love and sex. She knew that, despite her lack of experience.

Sterne loved her with exquisite slowness and tender thoroughness. Although his desire had been honed to razor-sharp intensity, he restrained himself every step of the way. His instincts urged him to thrust into her and gain the immediate release his body craved, but tonight he wasn't governed by his usual quest for quick physical satisfaction.

He thought of Brynn, of what she was feeling and experiencing for the very first time. He wanted to make it good for her. He watched her, he learned what pleased her, he savored her uninhibited responses to him. He'd never experienced such emotional intensity. Sex to him had always been quite basic. Arousal and satisfaction—his own—were all that had ever mattered to him.

Now Brynn's mattered more. Whatever had come before this was irrelevant. He'd had sex many times, but he felt as if this was the first time that he was truly making love.

Sterne caressed her intimately, and the rhythmic pressure of his fingers made Brynn feel wild and wanton. The last vestiges of control and thought spiraled away, and she moved against his hand, lost in a mindless haze of pure sensual pleasure. A tightness grew and grew within her, gathering force until it exploded like a sky rocket, hurtling her into a previously unknown dimension of sensation. Waves of pleasure radiated through her, leaving her limp and languid.

She opened her eyes slowly, to find Sterne watching her. She blushed. He smiled. "Good?" he asked.

"Yes," she said huskily, gazing up at him, smiling softly. "Very good."

"You're so passionate, so responsive," he said with a definite touch of masculine pride. He had loved every minute of her abandoned response to him. She made him feel sexy and powerful and proud to be the man who was her first lover. Her first and only lover. She belonged to him. The possessive, primitive thoughts filled his mind.

He kissed her, a long, slow kiss that swiftly escalated into fiery passion. He was throbbing with desire; he felt as if he would explode. He wanted her desperately. "Open for me, Brynnie," he whispered.

He held her hips and positioned her to receive him, then entered her slowly, inexorably. Her body arched and tensed, and she cried out at the sharp, tearing pain.

"It's all right, Brynnie. Relax." His words were punctuated with shallow breaths as he continued to press into her. "Oh, sweetheart, it feels so good. You're so hot and tight. You fit me perfectly, like a silk glove."

Brynn's eyes were open and she tried to breathe deeply. Perspiration beaded her forehead. She felt filled with scorching fire, stretched so tightly she feared she might rip apart. "Sterne," she gasped, trying to wriggle away from him. The slight movement seared her, and she immediately lay rigidly still. He stayed where he was, on her, in her.

Sterne felt as if he were in an unbelievably sweet, hot heaven. He was trembling with the force of his desire, of his pent-up need. Soon, soon . . .

"Sterne?"

Brynn's voice reached him on the heady sensual plane to which he had ascended. He forced himself to open his eyes and stared down at her. Her eyes were wide and wild. Though enveloped in a sea of exquisite pleasure, it occurred to him that she didn't seem to be sharing his feelings. Her face was bathed in perspiration, and she was visibly gritting her teeth. He was instantly concerned. "Brynnie, are you okay?"

She shook her head. "Oh, Sterne," she wailed softly. "It's—it's nothing like I thought it would be."

He could have taken offense. Her reaction was hardly flattering, definitely not a tribute to his skill as a lover. But Sterne wasn't thinking of himself. His attention was focused wholly on her. He decided that her frankness was endearing, far preferable to the lies and manipulation he and his past lovers had indulged in. His lips curved into an affectionate smile. "I knew I could count on you to be honest with me, Brynnie—even in bed."

A wave of tenderness surged through him. He wanted to comfort her and alleviate her anxiety. His own needs were placed on indefinite hold without another thought. "It'll get better, sweetheart, I promise." He kissed her lightly, his lips lingering and loving.

They lay together, their bodies joined. Sterne continued to kiss her and talk to her, his voice warm and reassuring. Brynn felt her body slowly begin to relax and accommodate itself to her lover. A hot buttery warmth replaced the initial tension, and she melted and flowed around him. She clasped her arms tightly about his waist and gazed into the dark blue depths of his eyes.

"Sterne, you were right," she said with a soft sigh. "It does get better." She dared to move a little. There was no trace of the previous pain. In fact . . . She moved again. "Much, much better." The sensations that were slowly building within her were incredibly pleasurable. She twisted beneath him as a burst of wildfire licked through her veins. She caught her breath on a moan of delight.

Sterne felt her response and his blood heated. "Oh, sweetheart," he breathed. He began to move gently, carefully. He'd told her it would be good, he'd said he would take care of her, and fulfilling those promises superceded everything else.

Brynn savored their closeness, the fullness of him inside her, the gentle and unselfish care he was taking with her. She knew it was atypical of Sterne to put anything ahead of his own gratification, yet he was doing exactly that, with her and for her. Her love for him swelled.

They moved together, desire and need burning between them, sending them both soaring higher and higher. Sterne thrust faster and deeper, and Brynn eagerly matched his rhythm. They raced toward the summit together, higher, hotter, until they both burst into flames, calling each other's names at the cataclysmic moment of ecstasy. . . .

For a long time afterward, they lay quietly together, limp and languid and nearly insensate with bliss. Sterne was the first to speak. "Sleepy?" he whispered, cuddling her against him.

"No." Brynn lifted his hand to her mouth and pressed his palm against her lips. She felt totally relaxed physically, but too emotionally high to sleep. "Sterne?" She raised her head a little to look into his eyes. "Is it . . . always like this?"

He managed a mirthless smile. The sweet euphoria that had enveloped him was fading. For some inexplicable reason, her question depressed him.

He was a veritable living encyclopedia on sex, yet making love with Brynn had transcended everything he had known before. Nothing in all his years of experience had prepared him for the shattering intensity of their lovemaking. It was as if their souls had met and merged along with their bodies, binding them spiritually as well as physically and emotionally. But how could he explain such a thing to her? For a moment, he panicked. Good Lord, he was beginning to sound like Spence and Patty! He settled for a prosaic, "No, it isn't always like this."

"It was wonderful." Brynn sighed dreamily. "Oh, Sterne, I love you!"

He tensed. "I know you feel you have to say that, honey." Damn, he didn't want to hurt her, but things were moving along at a rather alarming pace, he thought nervously. He could hardly believe what had happened between them tonight. Did he dare trust the uncharacteristic emotions that had surged through him, changing him from what he thought he was into someone he didn't know at all?

Brynn felt the sudden tension in Sterne. *Uh-oh*, she thought. Her dream lover had awakened and been transformed into a wary, anxious, confirmed bachelor. She suppressed a sigh. This wasn't going to be easy. "Poor Sterne." She continued to play with his fingers, but avoided his eyes. "You're wondering what a man says when the grateful virgin he's . . . uh, deflowered tells him she loves him."

He cleared his throat. "Brynnie," he began tautly.

"Sterne, stop worrying!" She hugged him impulsively. He had exhibited patience and tenderness and understanding during her moment of panic. Now it was her turn to do the same for him. "I'm not about to hit you up for a ring. I'm not heading out to register my china pattern or announce our engagement to the press. I'm" —she swallowed—"grateful to you for what you did for me tonight. I'll always remember tonight and I love you for that."

She was letting him off the hook, Sterne thought. He should be pleased. He should be relieved. She'd just changed her pledge of love to gratitude for a job well done. So why wasn't he pleased or relieved? Why was he feeling . . . cheated?

"You'd better go," she whispered, drawing away from him. She felt as if she were going to cry, and that would be truly terrible. Sterne would hate it if he were faced with an overemotional woman weeping over her "first time." No, she couldn't do that to him. "You can't risk falling asleep here. If someone should discover you in—"

"Are you throwing me out of your room?" The notion enraged him. He sat up straight. "You've used me as a convenient tool to relieve you of your virginity and now it's out the door? Is that it?"

She stared at him incredulously. "I thought you'd be thankful for the chance to escape."

"I don't want to escape! I'm staying here with you all night and if anyone in the family objects, too bad!"

"Stop shouting at me."

"I'm not shouting, you little idiot. I'm whispering. Can't you even tell the difference?"

She glared at him. "You may be whispering, but the tone is the same as a shout. And—and you're not staying here!"

"Yes, I am!" He glared right back at her. "Dammit, Brynnie, why are you trying to get rid of me?"

"Because you want to go. Don't try to deny it, Sterne. When I told you I loved you, you froze. I could almost *hear* you thinking, 'Lord, get me out of here!' Well, your prayers have been answered. You're free to go. I'm not going to try to make you stay."

"Oh, yes, you are. Because if you don't try to make me stay, I'll *make* you try to make me stay."

She shook her head, bewildered. "What?"

"I said I—" He broke off as the absurdity of his threat fully registered and sighed with exasperation. "Damn, I feel like a yo-yo. Up, down, down, up. I used to laugh at those poor jerks who spend their lives on an emotional Ferris wheel. I refuse to become one of them!" He flopped back against the pillows, scowling.

Brynn lay down cautiously beside him. "I don't like emotional Ferris wheels either."

He made a muffled exclamation of disbelief, but she noticed that he didn't withdraw from her or push her away. Her lips curved into a tender smile. "I wasn't trying to get rid of you, Sterne," she said quietly. "I really thought you wanted to go and I was offering you an easy way out."

He sighed again, then pulled her against him, tucking her into the curve of his right arm and shoulder. She curled up like a kitten, her warm soft body cuddling against his. "There isn't going to be any easy way out of this one, Brynnie. I can see that already."

She delicately traced the circle of his nipple. "Do you want out?" she asked carefully.

"Hell, no! Not yet, anyway." He laughed, a harsh, self-mocking laugh. "That's what makes it so . . ." He paused, searching for a word. "So damn . . ."

"Complicated," she suggested. She slipped one slender leg over his.

"Yeah. Complicated." His hand smoothed over the long, silken length of her thigh.

"I know what you mean." She reached up to kiss his chin. "I don't want out yet either."

Something about her words inflamed him. She didn't want out *yet*, she'd said. As if she would, someday. The thought was . . . unthinkable. And Sterne much preferred actions to thoughts, anyway.

He flipped over, pinning her beneath him, crushing her into the mattress. "It's damn lucky for you that you don't want out because—" His blue eyes glittered and he inhaled sharply. "I wouldn't let you go, even if you did."

His mouth closed over hers with fierce, demanding possession. "You're mine, Brynnie," he said hoarsely against her mouth. "You belong to me." His tongue traced her lips and he kissed her again.

"I know," she said frankly when he allowed her to

surface for air. She loved the feel of his heavy warm body upon hers. Her hands roamed over him, caressing his muscular shoulders, his broad back. Lying beneath him, it was easy to fit herself intimately to his hard contours. A sweet, hot thrill shot through her. The throbbing ache in her abdomen that had been eased to satiation only a short while ago, began to pulse again. She wrapped her legs around him.

Sterne's body hardened as arousal stormed through him. She felt so good beneath him, so small and soft and sensual. "Brynnie," he said with a groan. "I don't want to hurt you. . . ."

She smiled up at him, her pale green eyes alight with love and humor. "Oh, you won't, Sterne. After all, I can't be a nervous virgin more than once, can I?"

She worried him, and he stared down at her thoughtfully. She was still so innocent and she trusted him. A dangerous combination for a woman when it came to dealing with Sterne Lipton, and no one knew that better than he.

She closed her eyes and sighed with undisguised pleasure when he kissed her, and his concern for her grew. She was sweet and sincere and utterly lacked the manipulative skills necessary in handling a womanizing cad like himself. Why, he could count off the mistakes she'd made in just the past few minutes. She hadn't followed up on his lead and insisted that he was as much hers as she was his. She'd held a trump card there and hadn't even played it. And now . . . now she was offering herself to him again with openness and passion when she could be using the surrender of her virginity to wring guilty promises from him.

"Brynnie, honey, what am I going to do with you?" he asked rather desperately as she shifted provocatively against him. "I don't want to take advantage of you. . . ." But he had never wanted anyone like this, had never needed a woman with such an elemental, unmanageable force.

"You're not taking advantage of me, Sterne," she assured him, smiling up at him. "I can hold my own with you." Her eyes sparkled. "I can even best you. I've been doing it for fifteen years."

"Oh, have you?" He couldn't help but grin at her gleeful bravado. Memories flashed through his mind, and he saw himself and Brynn through the years, talking and teasing and fighting with each other. Somehow it seemed perfectly logical that it had all ended here, with them in bed together, talking and laughing, teasing and loving.

"Mm-hmm," she murmured. Her hands smoothed over his skin, and she luxuriated in the hard, smooth strength of him. She thought of how much she loved him and trembled with the force of that love. She wanted to prove to him just how much she cared, and as she well knew, actions spoke louder than words when it came to dealing with Sterne Lipton. "You said I belonged to you," she whispered softly, seductively.

"Yes," he said hoarsely. Their eyes held for one long silent moment.

"Then make love to me, Sterne." She opened herself to him.

"*With* you, sweetheart," he corrected her, his lips brushing hers as he spoke. There was a difference, he realized. He'd just never known it until now.

He filled her, hot and hard. She arched up to meet him and hold him deeply, tightly within her. They were a single unit, irrevocably joined. Brynn's mind spun out of control. "I love you," she cried as they moved together in a passionate frenzy. Waves of pleasure burst over her, and she clung to him.

This time Sterne didn't disclaim her breathless declaration. Emotion churned in him. She was his. No one had ever belonged to him before, but now he had Brynn, and it seemed natural and right—and even necessary—that she proclaim her love for him.

"I want you," he said as he felt himself explode with wild ecstasy. "Only you, Brynnie. Only you."

They lay together, naked and damp and warm and thoroughly sated in the sweet, langorous afterglow of fulfilled passion. Brynn sighed contentedly and snuggled against him. "You're mine," she said firmly.

Her tone brooked no argument. Not that it even occurred to Sterne to argue. He was unaccountably thrilled by the words she'd uttered. If no one had ever belonged to him before Brynn, the reverse was also true. He had belonged to no one. For years he'd operated as a single entity, not responsible or accountable to anyone but himself. He'd cared for no one and, conversely, no one had cared about him.

Which was exactly the way he'd wanted it, a sardonic little voice in his head reminded him. Until Brynn Cassidy had turned him inside out. Now he was panting for words of love and commitment from her. He'd even tried to lead her into saying them. She was hardly a trusting little innocent who needed protection from a rake like him, his alter ego proclaimed cynically. She was a master of the hunt who had baited and trapped him with accomplished ease.

"Sterne?" She was gazing up at him with concern in her love-softened eyes. "You're frowning. What are you thinking?"

He looked down at her and abruptly banished the snide thoughts circling through his head. She was gazing at him in a way that made him melt. He simply couldn't believe that she'd deliberately plotted and schemed to make him fall for her. She was his sweet and innocent little darling. "I was thinking that I don't want to go back to the city tomorrow." He kissed the top of her head. "The others will all be leaving but we could stay here for a while. Just the two of us."

She smiled at him. "It sounds wonderful, Sterne. But I have to be at work on Monday morning."

He frowned. "Can't you take some time off?"

She could, she thought. She'd accrued a number of personal days, not to mention her vacation. "How long?"

Sterne felt a momentary pang of irritation. He wasn't used to hearing anything but an immediate yes from a woman, to whatever he suggested. "A week," he replied, though he hadn't really given any consideration to a particular time frame. His time had always been his own, to do whatever he chose for however long he chose to do it.

Brynn thought about it for a moment. "I can probably take five days off this coming week. I'll call my boss tomorrow morning and find out, but I don't think there'll be a problem. Things have been pretty slow at the office this month, so I'm sure that—"

He silenced her with a kiss, not interested in hearing the logistics of her office scheduling. He would have her all to himself for a whole week. At the moment, that was all that mattered.

Sterne and Brynn planned to keep their newly altered relationship a secret from the rest of the Liptons. After all, they had less than one day—until Sunday night—before the family departed for their respective homes. They'd talked in bed and decided to play it cool and keep up the facade of old friends until they had the privacy to indulge themselves as lovers.

But at breakfast the next morning, they couldn't stop stealing glances and smiling at each other. They sat close together at the table and were unable to keep from touching each other. Sterne whispered private, sexy asides to Brynn that made her blush or giggle or playfully pinch him, and she whispered remarks to him that made him grin with an unmistakable glint in his eye.

Later at the beach, they spent an unusually long time rubbing sunscreen onto each other in the most thorough and sensuous way. They lay side by side on their towels talking, so completely absorbed in each other that neither even heard the children imploring

Brynn to help them build a sand castle. Eventually, the little girls left them alone and cornered Lucas into digging and construction.

In the water, Sterne found it necessary to lift Brynn over the high-breaking waves, and he held her long after the sea was calm again. And she couldn't help but splash him and tease him and cling to him after she'd successfully provoked him into grabbing her. Neither could resist kissing, on the sand and in the surf. And the kisses grew longer and more intense.

The whole family watched them speculatively and with varying degrees of concern. Stacey's expression bordered on downright alarm. Only Patty viewed the lovers with her usual tolerant serenity.

"I think our cover is blown," Sterne said as he and Brynn sauntered back to their towels after one playfully amorous dip in the ocean. The entire family was staring at them in silence, even the children.

"Do you mind?" Brynn asked, watching the family watch them.

"Me? Hell—uh, heck, no. Do you?"

He had been correcting himself every time he uttered a curse, and Brynn found it endearingly funny. He'd never minded swearing in front of her before. Over the years she'd heard him use language that would give even the saltiest sailor pause. But today, he wouldn't sully her ears with even the mildest expletive. She smiled at him. Today everything about him was endearing in one way or another. "I don't mind at all," she said truthfully. She was in love and exhilarated by it. She wanted to proclaim her love to anyone who would listen.

The first person she told was Stacey, who came into her room shortly before leaving for the airport that evening. "I can't believe I finally found you alone," Stacey said as she watched Brynn blow-drying her freshly shampooed hair. "Sterne's been sticking to you like Krazy Glue all day."

Brynn turned off the blow-dryer and smiled at her friend. "Stacey, I—"

"What time are you leaving to drive back to D.C. tonight, Brynnie?" Stacey interrupted, her tawny brown eyes troubled.

"I'm not driving back tonight, Stace." Brynn took a deep breath. "Sterne asked me to stay here with him this week and I told him I would."

"Oh, Brynnie!" Stacey's face crumpled. "I feel as if I'm watching you walk blindfolded across an eight-lane highway and not doing anything to prevent you from being hit."

Brynn smiled at the analogy. She couldn't help but smile at anything and everything today, she was so happy. And she wanted her oldest and closest friend to share in her happiness. "I'm in love with Sterne, Stacey."

Obviously, those weren't the words guaranteed to brighten Stacey's day. Her expression became even grimmer. "I can't believe it, Brynnie! After all these years—you know what Sterne's like, you've seen him at his absolute worst! And yet—"

"I've seen him at his worst and I've seen him at his best, too, Stacey," Brynn said quietly. "I know him. And I love him. Be happy for me, Stace. I feel wonderful. Happier than I've ever felt in my whole life."

Tears swam in Stacey's eyes. She put her arms around Brynn and hugged her tight. "I want you to be happy, Brynnie. But . . ." Her voice trailed off. "Just promise that you'll call me if you need me. Any time, day or night. Don't let the fact that Sterne's my brother stop you. Promise me, Brynnie, please!"

Brynn knew that Stacey was referring to the future, when Sterne would drop her and move on to another woman. It was a sobering thought. And a painful one. She couldn't bear to contemplate it. Not now when her love was so precious and new.

She pushed it from her mind. Why live in fear of

the painful future when the present held so much happiness and promise? She had a whole week alone with Sterne. She concentrated on that and resolutely refused to consider what lay beyond the next seven days.

Nine

Brynn and Sterne's week together in Rehoboth Beach was nothing less than a lovers' idyll. They spent seven days and nights alone, completely and intensely absorbed in each other. It was as if the rest of the world didn't exist. They swam and played in the water, they basked in the sun and took long walks along the beach. One night they drove to a seaside inn where they had a romantic, candlelight dinner. Another evening found them in a crowded, noisy seafood bar where they cracked crabs on a newspaper-covered table.

They talked endlessly, confiding secrets, vocalizing previously unspoken thoughts. Both relished the intimate sense of belonging exclusively to each other.

Their lovemaking grew more passionate, more meaningful, more deeply satisfying. They spent hours in bed, pleasuring each other, excitement and anticipation building and growing into an urgency that inevitably erupted into rapturous completion as they reveled in their mutual possession.

They stayed at the Liptons' beach house the entire

week. Sterne didn't suggest moving into his condo, and when Brynn mentioned visiting it, he abruptly refused. He didn't want her there, he realized. It had been the scene of too many excesses, too much wildness. The place held unsavory memories for him and he didn't want Brynn to be associated with it in any way. Their relationship was new and fresh and pure. It wasn't that he was ashamed of what had gone on in the condo, it was just that . . . Sterne stopped kidding himself. He *was* ashamed of what had gone on in the condo. And in his apartment in the city too.

When the week ended and he and Brynn returned to Washington, they continued to be inseparable. But they spent every night at Brynn's apartment, even though it meant moving out her narrow bed and replacing it with a new queen-sized one, bought and paid for by Sterne. He couldn't stand the thought of Brynn in his water bed, which had such an infamous history. He threw out the zebra and the leopard print sheets, but that hardly erased the scenes that had taken place in that bedroom.

Brynn playfully teased him about his apartment's custom-designed bathroom. She was curious, even eager, to explore it. Sterne strictly forbade it. That bathroom had a history, too, a notorious one, and he was determined that his Brynnie would not become part of it.

So they spent their time in Brynn's small apartment, and Sterne quickly became dissatisfied with the arrangement. It annoyed him that Brynn had only evenings and weekends free. She had an office to go to, Monday through Friday, from nine to five. He wanted her to stay with him.

"Why don't you quit your stupid job?" he grumbled early one Wednesday morning as he lay in bed and watched her dress for work. Wednesdays were particularly bad, he'd decided. It felt as if she'd been working forever, yet it was an eternity until the weekend.

Brynn adjusted the belt of her blue-and-white shirt-dress. "I can't quit my stupid job," she said. They had been through this before. "I've developed these annoying habits of eating and paying my bills. My stupid job enables me to do both."

"Ah, Brynnie, you know I'll give you whatever you need."

"The man wants to pay my electric bill," she teased. "How excruciatingly romantic."

"I'll show you what's excruciatingly romantic." He sprang from the bed and swept her up into his arms.

"Sterne!" she squeaked as he tossed her down onto the bed and lay on top of her. "I just finished putting on my makeup. My dress will get wrinkled, my hair—"

"Will be a mess," he finished for her, deliberately tousling it. "Now . . . on to wrecking the makeup and the dress."

"Sterne! I'm going to be late for work!" But her voice didn't carry the force necessary to stop him. In fact, it held a betraying note of laughter. She couldn't get angry with him for wanting to be with her. And the way he was kissing her neck and rubbing her breasts dissolved her already feeble protests into a soft moan.

"Maybe you'll get fired," he said hopefully as he unbuttoned the large blue buttons he'd watched her fasten just moments ago. "On the other hand, you can always tell your committee that you were working with someone close to the President. Maybe they'll think you're lining up funds for one of your projects."

"Maybe they will," she whispered, and closed her eyes as his mouth covered hers. She knew she was in no danger of being fired. The committee's hours were not rigidly fixed and she'd worked enough unpaid overtime to justify a slightly late appearance this morning. With a small sigh, she willingly gave herself up to the sweetness and the passion of their lovemaking. . . .

An hour later, her body still tingling and aglow, Brynn reapplied her makeup and brushed her hair. Her blue-and-white dress was hopelessly wrinkled, and she'd chosen a short-sleeved green cotton sweater and narrow white skirt to wear instead. Lying on the rumpled bed, Sterne watched her dress, his gaze possessive, his expression petulant.

"I want you to stay," he said bluntly. He sat up, his face brightening. "We can have lunch at the new Chinese place and catch the matinee of that movie you've been wanting to see."

She smiled at him. "You remind me of a little kid who's bored to death during summer vacation because all his friends are away and he has nothing to do." She crossed the room to sit beside him on the edge of the bed. "You know what, Sterne? You *are* bored. You need something to do."

He lifted her hand to his mouth and pressed his lips against her palm. "I have something to do and someone to do it with. You. And I'm never bored when I'm with you." That fact never ceased to astound him.

"Sterne." She framed his face with her hands. How to make him understand? "I love you and I love being with you. But you're not the only thing in my life. I have a job I like and friends I enjoy. You need that, too, darling. One person can't be all things to another. I can't be your occupation and your hobby and your sport, as well as your lover. If we were alone together twenty-four hours a day, day in and day out, we would—"

"We were alone together twenty-four hours a day at Rehoboth Beach," he interrupted testily. "I didn't notice you complaining."

"I loved every minute of it, Sterne. It was an idyllic interlude, which is what a vacation should be, and we enjoyed it to the fullest, knowing that it was temporary, a special time. Maybe that's *why* we enjoyed it so much. But for everyday life, you need something more. You need work, you need a productive outlet. You need something to do, Sterne."

"I have Sterne's Place," he reminded her. "It's open from four in the afternoon till two A.M. Are you suggesting that I spend my nights there, doing something . . . productive?"

"No, I don't want you hanging out there. I hate that place, you know that. I—I wish you'd sell it. I wish you'd sell both bars."

His brows drew together. "Do you?"

She nodded vigorously.

He shrugged. "I might." He didn't bother to add that if he had been bored with the bars before, he now found the thought of them intolerable. He had no desire ever to set foot in either place again. "I was damn—darn good with the accounting, though," he said thoughtfully. "I actually enjoyed doing the books. I have a real head for figures." He immediately clamped a hand over her mouth. "And I don't want to hear any witty double entendres from you, lady."

Brynn's eyes danced and she kissed his hand. "I wouldn't dream of uttering one."

"So." He pulled her into his arms. "Maybe I should consider doing something involving numbers. Accounting and banking don't particularly interest me, though." He thought for another minute. "Maybe I'll be a tax attorney."

"You?" She burst out laughing.

"What's so funny?" He scowled. "You don't think I can get into law school? Hey, if teenage actresses can get into places like Yale and Princeton, any law school in the country will welcome the President's son with open arms."

"I'm sure you're right, but . . ."

"You don't think I can make it through law school? Well, I can, Brynnie. I'm smart, I've always known that. I could've graduated from college *summa cum laude* if I'd gone to class and studied." He frowned. "I think I'd make a helluva tax attorney. And stop laughing! It's not funny!"

"It's just that I've always had this image of tax attorneys as conservative and, well, staid. Picturing you in a dark suit, somberly handing out advice on estate planning"—she paused to grin—"is pretty far out, Sterne. You have to admit that."

"That does it." He threw back the sheet and sprang from the bed. "I'm calling every law school in the area today. We'll see who has the last laugh, Miss Cassidy."

After Brynn left Sterne thought a lot about what she'd said. He did need something to do with his time, the time he didn't spend with her. What did he used to do with his days, before Brynn entered his life? he wondered. And remembered.

He'd spent his days sleeping off the nights before. He didn't get out of bed until late afternoon, and then only to begin the wild, frenetic cycle of nighttime excesses all over again. No wonder he'd never had to consider what to do with his days. Until these weeks with Brynn, he hadn't *had* any days!

But now he did, and he was filled with a newfound determination not to waste any more of his time. He spent the next week filling out applications and beginning to study for the LSATs, which he would take in September. Next came a series of negotiations involving the sale of Sterne's Place and Sterne's Place Two.

However, he still felt at loose ends during the day while Brynn was at work. It was her little apartment that was driving him crazy, he decided. The place was too small. He couldn't keep all his things there and consequently had to keep making trips back and forth to his own apartment, under Agent Rivington's watchful eye.

"We need more space, Brynnie," Sterne stated firmly one evening. "Especially in the fall when I start law school. I'm going to need a room to study."

"Sterne, you haven't been accepted by any law school yet," Brynn felt compelled to remind him. He seemed actually serious about becoming a tax attorney—she was still reeling with astonishment over that—but she worried that he might not be admitted to law school. She couldn't bear for him to be disappointed. She wanted him to prepare himself for that possibility, but Sterne refused to consider it.

"Of course I'll be admitted," he said. "It'll be up to me

to choose among them. Now, about this apartment . . . It's too small, Brynnie. It makes me claustrophobic. I want a house."

She stared at him. "A house?"

"Yeah. We have an appointment with a realtor on Saturday. You'll notice that I took your working hours into account and didn't chauvinistically schedule our house-hunting during the week."

"You want to buy a house?" Brynn was incredulous. Sterne Lipton, a home-owner? Dealing with such issues as mortgages and crabgrass and weather stripping? In her wildest dreams, she couldn't picture Sterne in such a scenario. Then again, she was having difficulty visualizing him as an upright tax attorney too.

"I'm not interested in the suburbs," he went on enthusiastically, "but I thought one of those big old houses in northwest Washington would be great. We can have a big yard with lots of trees and still have an easy commute—you to the Hill and me to law school."

"I'll go with you to look at houses if you want, but I'm not moving, Sterne. My apartment suits me just fine." Brynn was nervous and more than a little unsure of herself and of Sterne. He seemed to be changing in so many ways, and yet . . . She swallowed heavily. Sterne was not noted for the longevity of his relationships. As of now, she'd lasted longer with him than any other woman ever had. But did she dare give up the security of her own apartment and move into a house with him?

She glanced up and found Sterne watching her intently. "You're scared, aren't you?" he asked in the sardonic tone she'd heard him use so often through the years. "You think I'm going to get tired of you and throw you out, and then you'll have to contend with finding and moving into a new apartment along with coping with the breakup."

His words rankled. She didn't care for the images they evoked. "Maybe I'll get tired of you first," she retorted hotly, "and I'll want a place of my own, so I won't have to listen to you begging me not to break up with you."

"Baby, I can promise you this—I will never, ever beg you not to break up with me. I'll be gone before you even begin to realize that you want out."

"And how will you know that?" she challenged.

"I'll know." He glared at her.

She glared right back. "Do you want out now?"

"Do you?"

"I asked you first."

Anger surged through Sterne. Pride told him to walk out the door, but something else—he had no idea what it was—kept him where he was. "Are you trying to make me leave, Brynn? Because if that's what you want—"

"Of course it's not what I want!" Her eyes filled with sudden tears. "You're the one who started talking about getting tired of me and breaking up."

"And you're not the type to react passively to such threats. If someone takes a swipe at you, you strike right back." His lips curved into a wry smile. "Which is just what I need. I know I'm a heel. I'll walk all over anyone who lets me. I need someone to stand up to me." He took a step toward her and held out his hand. "I need you, Brynnie."

"Does this mean that you're not tired of me—yet?" she asked coolly. He could hurt her so much, she thought. Most of the time she suppressed the awareness of her terrible vulnerability to him, but tonight's little spat had brought it miserably to the fore.

"I'm sorry," he murmured, looking at the ground. "I didn't mean to hurt you."

"Oh, you meant to, all right," she said. "And you know exactly what will hurt the most."

"You hurt me, too, Brynn," he blurted out. They stared at each other in shock. Sterne couldn't remember the last time he'd allowed someone to cause him pain. For him to admit to being hurt by anyone was completely out of character.

"I—I did?" she whispered.

"I wanted you to want the house with me," he admitted, not meeting her eyes. "Instead, you told me you wouldn't leave your damn apartment."

His reluctant confession touched her. "I'm sorry I hurt you, Sterne." She put her arms around him and laid her head against his chest.

"I am, too," he murmured, his lips brushing her silky hair. His hands glided over her hips. "Let's officially end this fight and make up right now."

She stood on tiptoe to kiss his cheek. "That's the best idea I've heard all night."

He scooped her up and carried her into the bedroom. She hadn't, he noted, agreed to move out of her apartment and into a house with him. But when she smiled up at him, he smiled back and said nothing, not wanting to stir up another argument.

Sterne hadn't said the words she'd desperately wanted to hear, Brynn thought as he gently set her on her feet beside the bed. He hadn't told her that he wouldn't ever tire of her, that he found the idea of breaking up with her totally unthinkable. But when he kissed her, she clung to him and said nothing, not wanting anything to interfere with their loving reconciliation.

Sterne decided that Brynn needed another reason for moving in with him. An irresistible one. While she was at work the next day, he drove to a pet shop and bought an eight-week-old blond cocker spaniel. He greeted her at the door of her apartment when she returned from the office that evening, the puppy in his arms.

"For you, darling." He dumped the little dog in her arms.

Brynn was stunned. The puppy whimpered and tried to bury his face in the crook of her elbow. She stroked his soft fur and fell instantly in love.

"Do you like him?" Sterne asked eagerly.

"Oh, Sterne, he's adorable. I've always wanted a dog."
Her father had never permitted her to have one, though,
and since she'd grown up, she'd always lived in apartment buildings with regulations against pets. In fact,
she was living in one now. But she forgot all about
such rules and restrictions when she held the warm,
furry little body in her arms.

"I wanted to get you something special, to make up
for last night," Sterne said ingenuously. "I looked at
china dogs and toy dogs and then it occurred to me—
Brynnie should have the real thing. So I went to the
pet shop and this little guy kept looking at me with
this please-take-me-home expression. I couldn't resist.

The puppy squirmed in Brynn's arms, then licked
her with his little pink tongue. He gazed up at her with
big, soft brown eyes. "What a beautiful little fellow you
are," she crooned. "You're just the sweetest little puppy
in the world."

"I bought him a dog bed and some puppy food and
his own dish." Sterne took Brynn's arm and dragged
her into the living room to see. "And some toys too.
Look how cute he is with this little stuffed mouse."

"A mouse? Sterne, that's a cat toy."

Sterne held out the toy and the pup snatched it
between his tiny teeth and shook it fiercely from side
to side. Brynn and Sterne laughed in delight. "The
little squirt thinks he's a cat," Sterne joked.

"Squirt? That's a terrible thing to call such a precious puppy. His name is—is—" She stared thoughtfully at the little dog. "His name is Honeypuff."

"Honeypuff?" Sterne was appalled. "You can't call a
male dog Honeypuff. It'll have an adverse psychological
effect."

Brynn was undaunted. "And we can call him Honey
for short."

Sterne groaned good-naturedly. "Well, I guess since
he's your dog, Honeypuff it is."

Brynn held the puppy on her lap during dinner, and
she and Sterne spent the rest of the evening playing

with him. When the little dog finally fell into an exhausted sleep, Brynn laid him in the cushioned dog bed that Sterne had placed in a corner of the bedroom.

Brynn and Sterne were both deeply asleep, relaxed and replete from an intensely passionate session of lovemaking, when Honeypuff awakened, refreshed from his nap—and bored with being alone in the dark. His whines soon escalated into a series of attention-getting little barks.

Sterne woke slowly. "What's that?" he mumbled groggily.

Brynn rubbed her eyes. The puppy yipped again. "It's Honeypuff!" She scurried over to the dog bed and picked the small dog up. His barking and crying immediately ceased, and he wagged his tail and licked her face joyfully.

"He was lonely!" she exclaimed, and carried him over to the bed. She slipped under the covers, cuddling him. But Honeypuff didn't want to go back to sleep. He wanted to play. And he let his new owners know it, in no uncertain terms.

"Is this what having kids is like?" Sterne asked. He groaned and rolled onto his stomach, pulling the pillow over his head.

"Oh, I hope so." Brynn was entertaining Honeypuff with a rolled-up sock. She was completely enchanted with the feisty little puppy.

"Just make sure you get him to that newspaper in the kitchen in time," Sterne grumbled from under the pillow. "I don't want any doggie accidents in my bed."

"Don't mind Daddy, Honey. He's just a big grouch at three o'clock in the morning."

"Daddy?" echoed Sterne. "Me?"

"Of course you're Honeypuff's daddy. And I'm his mommy. We—uh-oh!"

"Oh, no!" Sterne jumped out of the bed. And began to swear.

"Oh, Sterne, don't overreact." Brynn was laughing. "It's just a *little* accident. After all, he's only a baby.

Here, you take him into the kitchen for a snack and I'll change the sheets."

Muttering under his breath, Sterne stumbled into the kitchen with the puppy. "I never used to be a zombie at three o'clock in the morning," he told Honeypuff as he prepared the puppy's food. "I used to be an incorrigible party animal and these were my hours to do it all. And now here I am, keeping regular hours—and daddy to a dog who uses my bed as his alternate bathroom. . . ." Sterne shook his head. "So what's next, Honeypuff? Sorry about the name, by the way. I'd have given you a macho name like Killer. What happens next?"

Brynn came into the kitchen, her arms full of sheets. "Next, I find a place that permits dogs," she said as she dropped the sheets in the washing machine. "The lease here strictly forbids pets of any kind."

Sterne wrapped his arms around her waist and hauled her back against him. "That's where the house comes in." He nuzzled her neck. "I want you to help me pick out a place and move in with me, Brynn."

Her heart began to pound. "Sterne, I—I just don't know."

"I'm living with you here. What's the difference?"

"There *is* a difference, Sterne." She bit her lip. "It's hard to explain, but this is my apartment and you have your own place, even if you're here most of the time. But moving into a house—your house—with you . . ." Her voice trailed off. "There's a difference to me," she finished softly.

Sterne sighed. "I suppose it stands to reason that a woman who stays a virgin for twenty-seven years isn't a likely candidate for living with a man without the benefit of holy matrimony."

She pulled out of his arms and turned to face him. "Don't, Sterne."

"Don't what? Don't speak the truth? You're holding out for a ring, baby. There's no need for you to deny it. At least you've been honest and up-front about it. The night of the Kayes' party you told me how much you wanted to get married. At that time your intended target was nice, normal, marriageable Dr. King."

"And you're implying that my current intended target is you?"

"Sweetheart, we both know it is."

Brynn took a deep breath. "All right, I'll be honest and up-front about it. Yes, I'd marry you. I love you, and I think in your own way you love me too. I think we could be very happy together. But you don't want to get married. You've never led me on with false promises. I've known all along that you don't consider yourself a marrying man."

She slipped into his arms. "Let's just enjoy what we have now," she murmured softly, soothingly. "I'll go with you on Saturday to look for a house, and meanwhile, I'll find myself an apartment that allows pets." She raised her face for his kiss. "There's no need to rush into anything or make any rash decisions. We're friends and we're lovers. That's enough for now."

Sterne kissed her. He knew he should be feeling relieved. She was putting no pressure on him, she wasn't forcing him into anything. So why was he feeling dissatisfied? It occurred to him that *he* should have been the one to say what she'd said, about not rushing into anything, about not changing the status quo. But he hadn't said it, he hadn't even thought it. *She* had.

An incredible thought struck him. Didn't Brynn want to marry him? She said she did, but . . . He knew very well that people often don't mean what they say. Or say what they mean. He certainly didn't, much of the time.

Brynn picked up the puppy and cuddled him close. "I think he's ready to go back to sleep, Sterne." She held out her hand to him. "Let's go to bed."

He took her hand. They were halfway to the bedroom when he suddenly demanded, "What do you mean, 'I love you in my own way'? What kind of a crack is that? Are you implying that my way isn't as good as somebody else's way?"

She shrugged. "It's just different, that's all. But that's okay," she added quickly. "I understand and I accept it."

"Oh, hey, that's big of you!"

"Sterne, there's no reason to get angry. You don't have to panic. I know you don't want to get married and I'm not going to push you into it."

"Why not?" he snapped. "Because my own way of loving isn't good enough for you?"

She almost giggled, but one quick glance at his dark expression stifled the urge. "It's late, Sterne, and we're both exhausted. Let's just go to sleep now."

They put the puppy in his bed, then climbed into their own between crisp, clean, pale peach sheets. Brynn closed her eyes and fell asleep almost immediately. Sterne lay awake, tossing and turning until dawn streaked the sky.

Ten

"You'll never guess what!" Brynn cried excitedly as she rushed into the apartment the next evening. Sterne was stretched out on the sofa and Honeypuff lay on his stomach, gnawing a small rubber bone.

She hurried over to the sofa and knelt beside it, giving Sterne a quick kiss and Honeypuff a fond pat. Sterne's heart turned over at the sight of her and a rush of pleasure surged through him. He'd missed her all day. It was as if his life was put on hold until she appeared. Everything began, everything mattered when she was with him.

"What'll I never guess?" he asked, clasping his hand around the nape of her neck.

"I got a list of places that allow pets," she said breathlessly, "and it's the most amazing coincidence, Sterne. Your apartment building is on the list! So when you buy your house, you can sublet your apartment to me and Honeypuff and I can move into it."

"What?" Sterne sat up, tumbling the puppy to the sofa. "How do you intend to afford the rent, Brynnie?

It costs a lot more than what you pay here. Nearly double."

"Double?" She sighed with disappointment. "Well, I guess that's out. I'll start calling the other places tomorrow."

"There's an alternative, of course." He caressed her neck with his fingers. "You and the pup can move into the house with me, rent-free."

It was a tempting offer, Brynn admitted to herself. She wasn't looking forward to the hassle of finding another apartment at an affordable rent. And, being perfectly honest with herself, she liked living with Sterne. She loved it. She loved him.

Sterne watched the emotions chase across her face. She was weakening, he was certain of that. He felt extraordinarily pleased with himself. He pulled her onto his lap, and his lips claimed hers. Her mouth opened for him, inviting the deep, hot penetration of his tongue.

Sensual spasms shuddered through her. "I love you," she whispered in a voice husky with emotion.

He stood up with her in his arms and strode into the bedroom. "I love you too," he said, then added lightly, coolly, "in my own way, of course."

It hurt for just a split second, then Brynn rallied herself. At least Sterne was being honest with her. He was telling her that he cared, but that his wasn't a forever kind of love. He was not, after all, a marrying man, and he was wise to keep reminding her of that fact. Otherwise, it would be so easy to delude herself into hoping, into believing that he . . . that they . . .

They heard a faint whine as Sterne closed the bedroom door. Honeypuff had followed them and was not pleased when he was denied admission to the room.

"Maybe we should let him in," Brynn suggested when the puppy's howling persisted.

"No way. He's got to learn to entertain himself, at least some of the time." Sterne had unbuttoned her apricot blouse and was working on the matching skirt with deft fingers.

The whining ceased as Honeypuff became bored and went off exploring. And it was silent in the bedroom except for the irregular breathing and sensual movements, the soft murmurs and moans of a man and a woman passionately making love.

"Hi, Riv," Brynn called as she waved to the Secret Service agent. He'd followed them to the big, gingerbread-style house in upper northwest Washington, where Sterne had arranged to meet with the real estate agent.

"Hi, Brynn," Rivington joined them, and reached out to pet the puppy in Brynn's arms. "Is this little fellow still keeping you awake at night?"

She shook her head. "Not since we put the stuffed animal and the alarm clock in his bed, as you suggested."

They were joined at that moment by an attractive middle-aged woman who introduced herself as Ginger Stroud, the real estate agent. Leaving Honeypuff in the front yard, under the supervision of the junior security agent, Sterne, Brynn, and Rivington followed her into the house.

"You're mighty chummy with Rivington these days," Sterne muttered to Brynn as Ginger Stroud extolled the virtues of the octagonal dining room. Since Brynn and Sterne obviously were involved in a private conversation, Rivington politely replied to Ginger's remarks.

"I chat with Riv every time I come or go from the apartment," Brynn whispered back. "If you'd stop treating your agents as if they were invisible and get to know them, you'd find that they're very nice guys."

"I treat them as if they're invisible because I wish they were invisible. I wish they weren't there at all. I hate being tailed wherever I go."

He hadn't minded the agents' presence nearly as much, though, since he'd taken up with Brynn, Sterne admitted to himself. Why? he wondered. Because he was now involved in wholesome pursuits such as applying to law schools, buying puppies, and viewing houses—with a respectable young woman who had the agents' wholehearted approval. Lord, was he actually beginning to conform to society's expectations? It was a sobering realization, but not nearly as revolting as he once would have thought. In fact . . . A smile slowly spread across his face as he slipped his arm around Brynn's slender waist and drew her closer. It wasn't revolting—or sobering—at all.

The house had three stories with six bedrooms, three baths, spacious living and dining rooms, and an enormous, fully modernized eat-in kitchen. A wood-panelled family room and a screened back porch had been added recently by the current owners. Both the front and back yards were wide and attractively landscaped and shaded by a number of huge old trees.

Brynn loved the place and listened intently as Ginger Stroud enthusiastically described every feature. She and Rivington frequently exchanged comments with the real estate agent. Only Sterne was silent during the entire tour. He finally spoke when they'd finished and were standing on the front porch, which ran the length of the house.

"Okay, I'll take it," he said succinctly.

Brynn, Ginger Stroud, and Rivington gaped at him.

"Mr. Lipton, this is only the first house on our list," the real estate agent said, recovering herself. "There are six more that I thought you'd be interested in seeing."

"I like this place. And I don't think I can stand traipsing through six more houses." He turned to Brynn. "You like this house, don't you, Brynnie? You and Rivington seemed nuts about the place while we were touring it."

"It's an excellent location, a fine neighborhood, and an ideal house for raising a family," Rivington said with a pleased little smile.

Sterne raised his brows and turned to Brynn. She flushed, and resisted the urge to deny that she and

Rivington were co-conspirators in some devious plot to domesticate Sterne Lipton.

"I love it," she said honestly. "But don't you think you ought to *look* at the other places at least?"

"Why?" He shrugged and turned to Ginger Stroud. "So where do I sign? We want this house and we'll pay whatever we have to to get it."

We, Brynn thought. Her heart jumped. Had Sterne actually begun to think in terms of *we* instead of his usual *I*?

Ginger Stroud was beaming. This was undoubtedly one of the easiest sales she had ever made. "I'll contact the owners right away and draw up a sales agreement this afternoon, Mr. Lipton."

Sterne took Brynn's arm and led her down the front walk to the sidewalk. Honeypuff tumbled across the grass to meet them. "The dog seems to approve," Sterne said as Brynn picked up the eager puppy. "And Ginger approves and Rivington approves. What about you, Brynnie? Are you happy about the house?"

She met his eyes. "It's a beautiful place," she said carefully.

"Yeah, yeah. And it's an excellent location in a fine neighborhood," Sterne added impatiently. "You sound like Ginger Stroud—or Rivington. You know what I'm really asking, Brynnie. Will you live here with me?"

She moistened her lips with her tongue. The little dog wriggled in her arms and she stroked the top of his head with her cheek. "Sterne," she began. She didn't know what she was going to say. Her thoughts and emotions were a confused jumble ranging from anxiety to exhilaration.

But before she could formulate some sort of reply, Rivington and the other agent positioned themselves between Sterne and a tall, dark-haired man who was approaching. Brynn drew in a sharp breath as she recognized him.

He was Cord Marshall, Washington's infamous muck-raker, the television reporter whose gossipy local talk show had been syndicated and was now broadcast all over the country. In addition to the weekly show, Marshall also wrote, twice a week, a syndicated column filled with the rumors, innuendos, and tidbits of nasty gossip he'd become famous for. At those rare times when there were no new rumors, innuendos, and nasty gossip, the undauntable Marshall simply made things up. He lived by the public's acceptance of the credo, *Where there's smoke, there's fire.*

Brynn scowled as Marshall's disagreeably familiar figure drew nearer. She'd had several run-ins with him in the past, thanks to his investigation of Stacey in her single days. Brynn still hadn't forgiven him for going through their garbage in his sleazy quest for information. And she knew that Marshall hadn't forgiven her for saturating his TV dressing room with skunk oil, either.

"I'm unarmed, gentlemen," Cord Marshall said. He held out his hands, palms up, and smiled at the Secret Service agents. "I only want to ask Sterne a couple questions."

Sterne frowned. "What do you want, Marshall?"

Marshall glanced from Sterne to Brynn. "So my informant was right. You're looking at houses, eh, Sterne?"

"I'm going to buy this one," Sterne said. "Hardly your kind of story, Marshall."

"That depends on what can be done with it." Marshall glanced briefly at the house. "It's a nice place," he said with a perfunctory, polite smile. Then he turned to Brynn and every trace of politeness evaporated. "And you'll be moving in with him, won't you, Ms. Cassidy?"

"That's none of your business, Marshall," she snapped.

"Wrong, doll. It's very much my business. I've been waiting for years to get something on you, and your squeaky-clean lifestyle has foiled me at every turn. But patience is a virtue of mine, and look what I've got now. You're the latest lover of the president's—shall we say, notoriously amorous?—son. Oh, yes, angel-face, it's my business, all right." Marshall grinned nastily.

"Leave her alone, Marshall." Sterne took a threatening step toward him, his eyes flashing blue fire. "And get the hell out of here before I rearrange your face."

Marshall took a few prudent steps backward, but didn't leave. "Is it true you're pregnant, Ms. Cassidy?"

"No, it's not true, you lying slime!" Brynn retorted hotly.

"Mmm-hmm. But isn't it true you were seen entering an abortion clinic down in southeast Washington last week?" Marshall fired back. "So you're no longer pregnant, eh?"

Brynn put down the puppy and started toward Cord Marshall, her fists clenched. "You rotten liar!" she said furiously. "I'll— "

"Upon being questioned, Ms. Cassidy flew into a blind rage and attempted to attack this reporter with her fists," continued Marshall with the fluent delivery of a war correspondent reporting from the battlefield.

Sterne caught Brynn's arms and pulled her back against him. "Marshall, those are outright lies and you know it. She could sue you for libel if you—"

Marshall laughed. "Do you know how difficult it is to win a libel suit, Lipton? Anyway, I can always plead a case of mistaken identity at that clinic, can't I? As for the pregnancy story . . . Well, she's your lover, isn't she? When sex is involved, the possibility of pregnancy is always legitimate speculation."

Sterne felt as if he'd been kicked in the head. He'd lived in the public eye long enough to know that lies and even idle speculation could damage reputations, could ruin careers. And Marshall had scored one depressingly accurate point. Once it was known that Brynn was Sterne Lipton's lover, she would be considered fair game for the worst kind of idle speculation. His past lovers weren't known for their sterling characters and Girl Scout virtues. And now Brynn Cassidy would be added to that list.

Sterne imagined Brynn's name being bandied about by sleazeballs like Marshall, and rage pounded through him. He couldn't let her be hurt like that. She was so good, so warm and loving. And innocent. But who would believe it if she were dragged through Marshall's sewer of slander?

Sterne's protective instincts surfaced fiercely, and his arms tightened around Brynn. He knew he would do whatever had to be done to protect her from any kind of harm, whatever the cost to himself.

"Brynn is not pregnant," he said through gritted teeth. "But if and when she becomes pregnant, it won't be a story for a muckraker like you, Marshall. It'll be announced through official White House sources." He took a deep breath. "Which is the way I intend to announce our engagement."

"Your engagement?" Marshall echoed. He stared from Brynn to Sterne in disbelief. "You're going to get married? *You*? Sterne Lipton?"

"Brynnie and I are engaged," Sterne said, nodding. "We've even started a family." He bent down to pick up Honeypuff. "This little guy is our first addition."

For a few moments, Brynn was too shocked to speak. She realized that Sterne was being chivalrous, and that alone was stunning enough to make her speechless. When had Sterne Lipton ever been concerned about anyone's reputation, including his own? He'd never cared what was said or printed about him. For him to make up this engagement story to protect her from Cord Marshall's lying innuendos . . .

"Sterne," she said, recovering her voice at last, "Marshall isn't going to keep this a secret, you know."

"You can bet on that," Marshall said, fairly salivating at the thought of this unexpected scoop. "The Good Girl lands the Rake. Morality triumphs, a rogue reforms. Middle America will love it!" He turned and dashed toward his car. "I'm airing the engagement story on my show tonight," he called over his shoulder.

"Sterne, do you realize what you've done?" Brynn

exclaimed nervously as Marshall drove away. "Cord Marshall is going to announce on national television tonight that we're engaged."

"Would you rather have him announce that you're my live-in lover? Or that you're pregnant? Or were seen near an abortion clinic?"

"The low-down, lying snake!" Brynn was livid. "Oh, Sterne, what are we going to do now?"

Sterne smiled slightly and wondered why he wasn't more upset. "I suggest we let ourselves be seen in a public place tonight, having dinner, drinking champagne, and looking for all the world like we're celebrating our engagement."

"But we're not engaged, Sterne!"

"And isn't Marshall going to look foolish when we deny that we are? We can say we were putting him on the whole time. Anything he'll try to say about us afterward will only come out sounding like sour grapes. And no one likes an ill-tempered reporter who can't take a joke."

Brynn nodded slowly. "You handled it very well, Sterne. It was . . . kind of you to protect my reputation." She felt strangely hollow inside and was painfully aware of the reason. She wanted the bogus engagement to be a real one. She wanted Marshall's announcement to be authentic, even if it meant that the garbage-scrounging snoop would have a genuine scoop rather than be duped.

"Should we call your family and warn them about Marshall's show tonight?" Brynn asked as she and Sterne dressed for dinner that night.

He shook his head. "None of them watch Cord Marshall's show, anyway. And they'll know that nothing he says is true, since they didn't hear it from us first."

"I guess you're right. I won't call my father or brother, either." She smoothed the skirt of her yellow polka-dot silk dress. It was sleeveless with a scoop neckline and a fitted bodice that flared into a bright full skirt. She was reaching for the short, matching jacket when Sterne's hands closed over her bare arms.

"You understand why I told Marshall what I did, don't you, sweetheart?" He inhaled the fresh, clean fragrance of her hair and couldn't resist dropping a kiss on the top of her head.

"Yes, Sterne, I understand." She moved away from him and slipped on her jacket. Not that his impromptu tale had really solved anything, she thought. It might protect her temporarily from Cord Marshall's vile insinuations, but if she were to move into the house with Sterne, if she were to live with him there . . .

Brynn knew right then that she couldn't do it. Much as she loved Sterne and wanted to be with him, she and Honeypuff would go apartment-hunting for their own place. Feeling a mixture of determination, unhappiness, and resolve, she turned to him. "Sterne . . ."

He put his arms around her. "This whole Marshall business has upset you, hasn't it, honey?" He kissed her temple. "Don't worry, it'll all be over soon."

"No, it won't. Not if I move in with you."

He stiffened. "Brynnie—"

"Not that it really has anything to do with Cord Marshall, anyway, Sterne. I'm afraid you were right when you said that a woman who stays a virgin for twenty-seven years isn't a likely candidate for a live-in relationship with a man." She laid her hands on his chest and gazed up at him.

Sterne stared into her eyes, at the sensual curve of her parted lips, and desire thudded through him. He drew her closer and felt the soft swell of her breasts against his chest, her thighs brushing his, and a thousand stunning, sensuous memories spun through him. Brynn laughing, teasing, fighting, and playing with him. Brynn, naked and warm and willing as he roused her from sleep with a kiss. Brynn lying down with him, opening her arms and her legs to him . . .

He wasn't going to give her up, he decided firmly. Nor was he going to let their lives be governed by her schoolgirl conscience. Frowning thoughtfully, he studied her face. "I suppose we could let Marshall's announcement stand," he said slowly.

Her eyes widened. "Let it stand?" she repeated bewilderedly.

She looked so small, so sweet and innocent, he thought. She was so trusting and sincere. He melted. His defenses crumbled when she looked at him in that certain way. "Oh, what the hell. Why not?" He picked her up and swung her around. "Let's make it real, Brynnie. Let's celebrate our engagement tonight."

She couldn't believe her ears. Just to make certain she wasn't having auditory hallucinations, she had to have him repeat it. "You mean we should . . . consider ourselves engaged . . . for real?" Her stomach lurched convulsively. "Engaged to be married?"

"There's no need to make a big deal out of it. We won't let it make any difference in our lives. We can give it a try and if it doesn't work out . . ." Sterne was speaking his thoughts aloud, in an attempt to reassure himself more than her. "If it doesn't work out, we'll just move on. No hard feelings. Okay, Brynnie?"

Hardly the proposal a woman dreams of, Brynn thought wryly. But then, it was something of a miracle that Sterne was proposing at all. He must really want her to live with him to take things this far. He actually must love her, even if he would only admit to it with the qualifying "in his own way." Would he ever admit to his deeper feelings? *Could* he?

"Okay, Brynnie?" he pressed.

She stared into the jewel-blue depths of his eyes. She loved him and she wanted to take what he offered her, whatever qualifying tag accompanied it. She wouldn't demand what he couldn't give, she promised herself. She draped her arms around his neck. "Okay, Sterne."

She kissed him then. Everything she wanted to give him was in that kiss. All her love and passion and loyalty. All her hopes and dreams. "I love you, Sterne," she whispered. She loved him much more than he could ever know.

They chose El Caribe, one of Washington's best sources of Latin cooking, for their celebratory dinner and feasted on paella, mariscadas, and a spectacular version of roast pork. They toasted each other with champagne so liberally that Rivington had to drive them from the restaurant back to Brynn's apartment. Nobody minded. The happy couple snuggled in the backseat while Rivington drove, smiling in avuncular approval.

"I have an idea," Sterne said as the big black Mercury glided through the Washington traffic. "Let's go on to Chevronne's for a nightcap." Chevronne's was a popular new nightspot in fashionable Georgetown. Brynn knew there was live music and dancing there, and the thought of dancing with Sterne was incredibly appealing. "Yes, let's," she said happily, cuddling closer to him. She and Sterne really were engaged! The incredible realization permeated her pleasant wine-induced haze and she glowed with joy.

Brynn and Sterne sat at a cozy table for two in a darkened corner of Chevronne's and toasted each other with more champagne between slow dances on the crowded dance floor. It was a special, romantic night, one Brynn knew she would always remember. Sterne was attentive and loving and seemed unable to keep his eyes or his hands off her.

He was patently uninterested in the sexy blonde who kept flashing him come-hither stares, or in the sultry brunette who sashayed over to their table, claiming a prior acquaintance and making it extremely obvious that she was willing to renew it anytime, anywhere. Sterne made it extremely obvious that he only had eyes for Brynn.

"Ready to continue our celebration in a more private place?" he asked huskily as they swayed dreamily to a slow, evocative song of love gone wrong.

She moved against him sinuously. "Oh, yes."

They kissed lightly, then turned to leave the dance floor, hand-in-hand. They were so wrapped up in each other that they promptly collided with another couple making their way onto the floor.

"Hello, Brynn. Hello, Sterne," the attractive blue-eyed blonde woman greeted them, giggling. "Small world, isn't it?" She giggled again.

Brynn recognized a very tipsy Laura Chambers. Laura's hair was tousled, her lipstick smeared. As Brynn said hello to Laura, the other woman turned to her escort, Kyle Zimmer, whose hand was resting possessively on her hip. Brynn was too full of goodwill tonight to bear ill will toward anyone, even the man who'd once bet Sterne he could get her into bed.

Sterne and Kyle exchanged wary nods.

"I haven't seen you since the night of the Kayes' party, Brynn," Laura said, and winked conspiratorially. "Remember our little heart-to-heart in the bedroom?" She swayed slightly and Kyle's other hand came around her waist to steady her. Laura wriggled provocatively against him.

Sterne took Brynn's hand. "If you'll excuse us, we were just leaving."

"Rumor has it that you two are dating," Laura interjected, halting their attempt to escape.

"Did you watch Cord Marshall's show tonight?" Sterne asked suddenly, a boyishly eager smile lighting his face.

"Lord, no!" Laura shuddered dramatically. "I make it a point never to watch that obnoxious insect's show. I'll never forgive him for the hatchet job he did on my father."

"Did Marshall do a number on you two?" Kyle asked Brynn with genuine interest.

"Well, not exactly," she said tentatively.

"He announced our engagement," Sterne blurted out. "And it just happens to be true. Brynnie and I are engaged." He sounded so happy, he looked so happy. Brynn felt her eyes fill with sentimental tears.

Laura and Kyle stared, their mouths comically agape in a classic expression of shocked incredulity. Then Laura burst into delighted laughter. "Brynn! My Lord, Brynn, you did it! You did it!" She clasped Brynn's shoulders and shook her playfully. "I owe you some sheets, don't I? Name the size and color and I'll have them delivered next week. I can't believe it! You actually went and did it!"

Looking embarrassed, Kyle murmured apologetically, "Er, Laura has had a bit too much to drink tonight. She's slightly incoherent."

"I'm not drunk!" Laura said indignantly, her slurred speech and wobbly stance belying her words. "Brynn knows what I'm talking about. Remember what I told you I wanted to do, Brynn? Maybe I should take lessons from you. What you've pulled off makes you a leader in the field."

"Laura, my sweet, you're not making any sense," Kyle told her in maddeningly patronizing tones. "Perhaps I'd better get you home."

Laura turned on him in a drunken fit of pique. "Brynn, tell him that I'm making perfect sense," she demanded crossly. "Tell him about our bet and how you've won it."

Brynn swallowed. "Laura, we—"

"No, *I'll* tell him." Laura cut her off, grinning giddily as she faced the two men. "The night of the Kayes' party, when you two made that miserable bet about getting Brynn into bed . . . well, you weren't the only ones making bets that night. Brynn and I made one ourselves. We bet that she could make Sterne Lipton fall in love with her—bring the bastard to his knees, so to speak. The payoff was a set of Pratesi sheets. But, Brynn . . ." Laura extended her arms and stumbled as she attempted to whirl around. "You've exceeded the terms of the bet. You actually got him to propose! I'm going to send you *two* sets of sheets! You've earned them." She leaned forward and caught Brynn's hand, pulling her closer to whisper confidentially, "When are you going to drop him? And how? *I've got it!* You can stand him up at the altar!"

"Laura, for heaven's sake!" Kyle groaned and yanked her to his side. "We're leaving," he announced, and dragged Laura off without a backward glance.

Brynn looked at Sterne, and her heart sank. His face was white, his lips drawn in a taut, straight line. His dark blue eyes glittered with rage. "So you and Laura made a bet, did you?" he said harshly. "And you won."

He looked positively murderous. Brynn gulped. "Sterne, Laura was drunk. She—"

"Knew exactly what she was talking about," he interrupted coldly. "And so did you, you little bitch. You bet Laura that you could get me to fall for you, and after I did, you planned to drop me flat."

Brynn stared at him. He was angrier than she'd ever seen him. And clearly in no mood to listen to reason. "Sterne, let's go home," she said in conciliatory tones. "We can't talk here and—"

"I'll be damned if I'll go anywhere with you, lady!" His voice lowered to a low, furious whisper. "I don't want to talk to you at all! Laura Chambers said everything there is to say." Sterne felt as if he were on fire. Rage licked through him. He was almost dizzy from the force of it. "I thought you were so sweet, so innocent! I worried about you. I wanted to protect you!" He didn't bother to add that he'd trusted her. It galled him too much to think how thoroughly he'd been had. "And you've been playing me along all the time—to win a bet! With a Chambers!"

"Sterne, there was no bet with Laura," Brynn said calmly. She wondered how she could sound so cool and collected when she was dying inside. Somehow she'd stepped out of herself and was both participating in and observing the scene. "You can't really believe that I'd do such a thing. I would never use you or hurt you in that way. I love you."

"Such a cool little liar." Sterne flung the words at her

through a haze of blind fury. "You're slick, Cassidy, I'll grant you that. You beat me at my own game."

"I wasn't playing a game with you, Sterne. I'm not playing one now."

"That's right, baby, because the game is over. And I'm dropping you before you can do it to me. Be sure to tell that to Laura. Maybe it'll cost you that extra set of sheets." He stalked through the crowd, weaving his way between the tables.

Brynn followed him, running to keep pace. She didn't know what else to do. She caught up to him at the door, and grabbed his arm. "Sterne, please, listen to me."

He shook her off. "Get lost, baby. It's all over."

"Sterne, no!" Brynn was unaware that her voice had risen and that people in the crowded vestibule were staring at them with avid interest. She felt as if she were caught in a nightmare. This couldn't be happening. Sterne couldn't leave her this way. They were in love, they were going to be married!

Rivington was beside them, looking completely confused. When Sterne started out the door, the agent paused to look at Brynn.

"She's not coming with me!" Sterne roared. The pain coursing through him was unlike anything he'd ever experienced. His thoughts crashed through his head, bludgeoning him until he felt as though he were becoming unhinged. Sweet, innocent, sincere little Brynnie was a fake and a liar. She'd used him! He had let her get closer to him than anyone ever had, he'd even tried to change his life for her, and she'd betrayed him. She never cared at all. She'd been laughing at him the whole time.

"Sterne, what's going on?" an exasperated Rivington demanded. The agent had managed to maneuver himself, Sterne, and Brynn out of the club and onto the sidewalk.

"I never want to see this lying bitch again," Sterne snapped.

"Sterne, please!" Brynn felt hot tears stream down her cheeks, but she didn't bother to wipe them away.

"Suddenly," Sterne said, "Cord Marshall's appearance at the house today makes perfect sense." She flinched at the contempt in his eyes. "You were the informant who told him when and where to show up. You arranged for him to make those accusations, knowing that I felt this—this idiotic urge to protect you. I thought you were so pure, so sweet and loyal and innocent! I even bought your reluctant-to-move-in-with-me act and played right into your hands by agreeing to make our engagement real. You and Marshall and Laura Chambers pulled off a real coup, Brynn. You made a complete fool of me."

"Lipton, you're a complete fool if you believe that imbecilic tale." Rivington's voice was a virtual growl.

But Sterne wasn't about to listen. He could hear nothing but tormenting thoughts of betrayal. For the first time since he was a small child and realized that his mother was never coming back, he felt tears burn his eyes. He was horrified by that unfamiliar moisture. Oh, no, she wouldn't reduce him to tears! Without another word, he strode to the black Mercury sedan and climbed inside, slamming the door.

The message was clear. Rivington had to accompany his charge and leave Brynn, no matter how much he regretted having to do so. "I'll talk to him like a Dutch uncle," the agent promised. "He'll come around, Brynn, don't worry."

She shook her head. "No, he won't. He doesn't trust me, Riv. He hates me." She tried to swallow around the huge lump in her throat. She felt as if she'd swallowed a ball of ground glass.

The car horn sounded, an impatient, angry blast. "The man's a total fool all right," Rivington said with feeling. "Do you have money for cab fare home?"

She nodded and resisted the urge to howl with pain. There was nothing for her to do but take a taxi back to her apartment, alone. Honeypuff greeted her at the door and she scooped him up in her arms and cried and cried, until the puppy was damp from her tears and yipping in protest.

Eleven

Brynn mused over the concept of fate as she lay in bed, staring at the ceiling. In certain stories and pictures, fate was personified, spelled with a capital F, and depicted as either a sinister villain in a black cape or a beautiful, capricious woman. But after last night's heartbreaking debacle with Sterne, and this morning's unexpected phone call, she decided that fate was really an idiot with indescribably bad timing.

How else to explain that her caller this dismal Sunday morning had been none other than Dr. Daniel King? When she answered the phone Daniel sounded determinedly cheerful—and a little uncertain. "I haven't talked to you in a while," he said.

Brynn's head was pounding, the result of too little sleep and too many tears. Her eyes were red and burning from an excess of salt, and her nose was stuffed. "How have you been, Daniel?" she managed to ask, and marveled at the strength of ingrained propriety. She wanted to slam down the receiver and weep, but good manners kept her on the phone, politely asking, "And how is Nicolette?"

There was a brief silence, then Daniel said hesitantly, "Brynn, I heard on Cord Marshall's show last night that you're engaged to Sterne Lipton. Is it true?"

"No," she said tersely. "It's not true, Daniel."

"Well, then." Relief was evident in Daniel's voice. "Would you have dinner with me tonight, Brynn? I realize this is awfully short notice. You may already have other plans," he tacked on hastily.

No, she had no plans for tonight, but to sit in her lonely apartment and miss Sterne. A fresh wave of pain assailed her. It hurt so much.

"Brynn, I'd really like to see you tonight." Daniel's voice on the other end of the line roused her from her melancholy reverie.

"Why, Daniel?" She asked wearily. "Where's Nicolette?"

"Who knows? Who cares? Not me."

"You broke up?"

"It was a mistake for me to have become involved with her in the first place. She's just a child, only twenty-one years old, you know. I much prefer mature women, like you, Brynn. Please have dinner with me tonight."

He sounded close to desperation. Suffering her own emotional wounds, Brynn was quick to perceive another's pain. She took a deep breath. "Dinner tonight will be fine, Daniel."

When the phone rang an hour later, Brynn pounced on it. It had to be Sterne! *Please let it be Sterne*, she prayed.

It wasn't. Stacey was on the line, phoning from her home in Cambridge. "Brynnie, you won't believe what Cord Marshall said on his show last night!" Stacey exclaimed without preamble. "I've had at least eight calls about it. Marshall tried to claim that you and Sterne were engaged!"

"I know," Brynn said. And then she burst into tears.

It was a long, wet telephone call. Between sobs, Brynn

told Stacey the whole story, from Laura's suggestion of a bet—which she had turned down at the beginning in no uncertain terms—to Sterne's suggestion that their bogus engagement be a real one. She had calmed down by the time she came to last night's dreadful scene with Sterne. Her voice was flat, her tone dead, as she described their terrible parting.

Stacey cried too. She stopped only when Brynn mentioned apathetically that Daniel King had called for a dinner date. "He was the nice, normal, marriageable doctor, wasn't he?" asked Stacey, brightening a bit.

"A pediatrician," Brynn said with a sad little sniffle. "I think he just broke up with his girlfriend."

"A pediatrician on the rebound!" Stacey definitely perked up. "Oh, Brynnie, this could be just what you need to help you put that rat of a brother of mine out of your head."

Brynn couldn't share her best friend's enthusiasm. She went through the motions of dressing for her date with Daniel, choosing a turquoise plaid cotton skirt and bright knit top, wishing all the while she was dressing for Sterne.

Daniel arrived, his smile as appealing as ever. He was wholesome and unthreatening, and Brynn tried to appreciate those good qualities as she ached for Sterne's dark, disturbing sexuality. They played with Honeypuff for a while, and Brynn had to concede that Daniel King was a nice man, fond of dogs and children. But he wasn't Sterne, and that meant he could never be right for her. Even if he was an eligible pediatrician on the rebound.

And he was very much on the rebound. During dinner, Brynn found herself putting her own pain aside to hear about Daniel's.

"It was a mutual breakup," he said over steaming bowls of French onion soup. "Nicolette is totally immature. I realize that now. She has this crazy idea that she should remain a virgin until she's married."

"How quaint," Brynn said dryly. "Naturally you tried to disabuse her of such a foolish notion."

Daniel missed the sarcasm in her tone completely. "Nicolette accused me of not respecting her values because I was always trying to get her into bed. And I accused her of sexual blackmail."

"Ah, yes, sexual blackmail," Brynn said sardonically. "The old holding-out-for-a-ring ploy." Sterne had accused her of that too. Oh, Lord, he'd accused her of so many hurtful things!

Daniel nodded earnestly. "We ended up fighting over it all the time. I couldn't take it anymore, Brynn. I'm thirty years old. I want a mature relationship with a mature woman, not a game of cat and mouse with a little tease." He leaned forward, his eyes intense, and took her hand.

Brynn stared at him, analyzing the situation with a dispassionate calm that surprised her. Timing, she thought. It was all a matter of timing. Daniel King was ready for a relationship, a serious one. And right now, he was feeling vulnerable and ill-used. It would be so easy for her to step in, to take him to bed and wipe all thoughts of sweet little Nicolette out of his head. Possibly, she could maneuver him into marrying her before he ever caught on to the fact that he didn't love her—and that she didn't love him.

If she were the conniving, heartless manipulator that Sterne accused her of being, she would do just that. But . . .

Brynn sighed. She didn't want Daniel King, no matter how easy it would be to land him in a weak moment. She was in love with Sterne Lipton and suspected she would be for a long, long time. She blinked back the tears that stung her eyes. There would be plenty of time to cry over her unrequited love. Right now, she might as well channel her energies into something constructive. Rivington had promised to talk to Sterne like a Dutch uncle. She would talk to Daniel like a . . . Dutch aunt?

"Daniel, if you expect me to condemn Nicolette for not hopping into the sack with you, you're in for a big surprise," she said succinctly, withdrawing her hand from his. "I don't think any man has the right to make a woman do anything she doesn't want to do. Furthermore, I think *you're* the one using sexual blackmail."

"That's not true!" he said, flushing.

"You're feeling guilty," she continued, "as well you should." She was beginning to enjoy herself. Taking Daniel to task was an effective outlet for some of the anger she felt toward Sterne and his appalling lack of faith in her. "I'm glad Nicolette broke up with you. I hope she'll soon find another man who'll appreciate her high standards and marry her."

She watched Daniel blanch and decided he was a rat, even if he was an eligible pediatrician on the rebound. He still cared for Nicolette, but had been perfectly willing to take another woman to bed to satisfy his own selfish desires. She glared at him, feeling decidedly hostile. "Nicolette will make a beautiful bride," she embellished nastily, "and some other man will have the pleasure of—of introducing her to passion." A bit overblown, she thought, but effective nonetheless. Daniel was looking sick.

"And she'll have beautiful babies," she added, letting him have it with a final thrust. "Maybe she'll bring them to your office, Daniel. Would you like being Nicolette's children's pediatrician? Every time you looked at them, you could imagine her in bed with another man—"

"Stop!" Daniel threw down his napkin. "I don't want to listen to any more, Brynn."

"Too bad, because I have a lot more to say."

By the time Daniel brought Brynn back to her apartment, he was thoroughly morose. Brynn found herself feeling sorry for him. Perhaps she had been a little rough on him. "Daniel," she said gently, "Nicolette hasn't married that other man yet. If you really care for her, why don't you give her a call? Maybe if you promise to quit trying to blackmail her into bed, she'll give you another chance."

She felt nothing but relief when Daniel shuffled out of her apartment—and out of her life. She was certain of that.

The telephone rang as she was getting ready for bed. She warned herself against the leap of anticipation that sent her heart slamming against her ribs. If it was Sterne . . .

It was her landlord, calling to say it had been reported that she had a dog, and reminding her of the building's restriction against pets. She had to get rid of the animal or leave the apartment. Brynn hung up and sighed. What a fitting end to one of the worst days of her life!

Three days. Sterne glanced at his calendar and then at his watch for confirmation. It had been three days since he'd learned of Brynn's betrayal. He couldn't eat, he couldn't sleep. When he realized that alcohol wasn't dimming his pain, he gave up trying to drink himself into oblivion. He thought of losing himself in the throes of sexual passion, but he couldn't bring himself to talk to another woman, much less make love to one.

He was hurting badly. All those years of successfully avoiding pain hadn't prepared him for the agony of losing Brynn. If he'd kept himself emotionally anesthetized before, the anesthesia had finally worn off—with a vengeance. He wondered how he was going to get through the next hour, not to mention the days and nights that were strung out endlessly before him. For the first time, Sterne realized how empty and meaningless his life really was. How alone he was. He had no one to share his grief, no one to offer a word of consolation or advice. He didn't have any real friends. He'd always been emotionally distant from his family. The only person who'd ever really cared about him, whom he could really talk to, was Brynnie. And now she was gone.

He didn't want to see her, he told himself. She wasn't what he'd thought she was. Then the memories would flood his brain, bittersweet memories of the times they'd spent together, and a terrible, sinking feeling would drag him down into a mire of despair. She hadn't been acting. He forced himself to admit the truth. She was everything he'd known she was, everything he ever wanted and needed in his life.

He had thrown it all away in a crazy moment of foolish hubris and appalling bad judgment. He'd displayed an unforgivable lack of trust and faith in her. When he thought of the things he'd said, of the way he'd treated her, he cringed with pain and regret. She didn't deserve to be treated that way, and he didn't deserve her. He saw no way out of the misery that plummeted him deeper and deeper into dark depression. Brynn would never forgive him for what he'd done to her. It was useless even to try to beg her forgiveness.

On the fourth miserable day after their breakup, Sterne could no longer stand his isolation. He needed to reach out to someone, but to whom? His father and stepmother? Never. For the first time, he wished he could talk to his brothers. Spence and Lucas might be very different from him, but he knew they cared. Unfortunately, they were both at the farm in Fredericksburg, and inaccessible. Spence and Patty had decided to live without what they called "the tyranny of the telephone."

There was his sister. He could call her. His hands trembled as he dialed Stacey's number. Stacey was the closest link he had to Brynn, and she had always been open to a closer relationship with her eldest brother.

"Stacey?" His voice shook when his sister came on the line.

"You!" Stacey banged the receiver down in its cradle.

Sterne was so surprised that he automatically dialed her number again. "Stace?" he said tentatively when she answered.

"I promised myself that I would never speak to you again, you—you miserable creep!" Stacey snarled. "But I'll make this one exception just to tell you what a disgusting, arrogant, worthless cockroach I think you are!"

He swallowed hard. "I guess you heard about Brynn and me."

"I don't even want to hear you speak her name! Of all the women in the world, you had to pick my best friend for one of your cheap, self-centered flings! She's the prettiest, funniest, smartest, sweetest person I've ever known, and you had to use her and then throw her away like yesterday's trash."

"It—it must look like that to you," he conceded glumly. "But . . . Oh, Lord, Stacey, I've made a mess of it! What am I going to do?"

There was dead silence on Stacey's end of the line. Finally, she spoke. "Is this really Sterne?" she asked suspiciously.

"Yeah, it's me," he replied with a harsh, self-mocking laugh. He didn't blame his sister for doubting it. When had he ever displayed regret or sorrow? When had he ever displayed genuine emotion? Stacey was used to dealing with a brother who was a self-involved zombie, not a real person.

"You hurt Brynnie badly," she informed him. "The least you owe her is an apology for those totally idiotic accusations you made."

"Do you think she'll forgive me?" he asked, casting aside all pride.

"I don't know," she said tersely. "But you'll never find out unless you ask her."

Honeypuff was sound asleep in Brynn's arms as she carried him from her car into her apartment building. She'd spent the evening at Mary Jo and Bernadette's apartment and it was nearly midnight, rather late for her to be out on a weekday night. But she'd been up late every night, spending each evening with friends. She was too extroverted to spend all her time alone crying over Sterne, but her suffering was no less intense. She was grateful to have friends who were willing to share her pain and fill her hours.

Honeypuff woke up as she mounted the final steps to her apartment. He barked. "Shh!" Brynn whispered. "All we need is for the neighbors to complain about a barking dog. We'll be evicted tomorrow!"

The landlord had been calling daily to inquire if Brynn had rid herself of the offending pet or made plans to live elsewhere. Brynn was stalling him, but she knew it couldn't last for long.

Honeypuff yipped again and began to wag his little tail. Brynn glanced around, wondering what had claimed the puppy's interest. Then she saw Sterne, standing in the shadows of the small hallway. Her heart jumped.

"May I come inside and talk to you?" he asked in a cautiously polite tone she'd never heard him use before. Her gaze moved over him. He was wearing a gray three-piece suit, a white shirt, and a navy-and-burgundy striped tie.

She'd seldom seen him dressed so conservatively, so formally. She was acutely conscious of her neon-colored shorts and T-shirt. "Yes, come in," she said.

"I came to apologize," he said stiffly when they were inside. "For all the irrational, rotten things I said, for—"

"I accept your apology," she interrupted swiftly. She set the puppy down on the rug and stared at Sterne.

"You do?" He was staring just as intently at her. "Just like that?"

She drank in the sight of him. She noticed the hollow circles beneath his eyes, the tense set of his jaw. He was pale and his stance was rigid. "Yes." She nodded and added encouragingly, "Anything else?"

Sterne's eyes widened. Did he dare to hope? He took a deep breath. She hadn't screamed at the sight of him. She hadn't cursed him and thrown him out. She hadn't made him grovel and then laughed in his face.

He ran his tongue nervously over his lips and his heart pounded against his ribs. "Would you . . . have dinner with me sometime?"

Her eyes filled with tears and she nodded again. "Yes. I'd like that very much."

He closed his eyes and began to shake. His whole body trembled and throbbed with the force of his emotions. "Oh, Brynnie, will you take me back?" he blurted out. "I'll do anything, anything you want—"

She flew across the room and in a split second was in his arms. "Yes, Sterne, yes! I love you." She was laughing and crying at the same time. "I've missed you so much."

He held her as if he would never let her go. He was dazed. The only reality was Brynn in his arms, holding him and telling him that she loved him. "I've been in hell," he said hoarsely. "Oh, Brynnie, I love you. And I was too stupid to realize just how much until I thought I'd lost you. Please, please, don't ever leave me."

"No, never." She stood on tiptoe and framed his face with her hands, then touched her mouth to his.

One of Sterne's hands slid up to cup her neck. The other spread across the small of her back, pressing her closer, and he responded fervently to her gentle kiss, deepening it. They kissed and kissed, their mouths clinging as the passion erupted between them.

"I thought I'd never kiss you again," Brynn confessed in a whisper when he lifted his mouth from hers. "Never hold you again, never talk to you again." She shivered at the heartbreaking thought.

His lips brushed hers. "I was a fool. No, worse." What had Stacey called him? He tried to remember. He'd felt it extremely apropros. "An arrogant cockroach."

"A *what*?" Brynn drew back, laughing. She felt lighter than air. She was floating in a bubble of joy.

He gazed down at her and his heart swelled with love. "I love you so much, Brynnie. And not merely in my own way," he added fiercely, his eyes blazing with love. "I want to love you in your way, generously and unselfishly and"—his voice dropped to a husky whisper— "with forgiving and understanding. Thank you, sweetheart, for understanding and forgiving me. For loving me."

She was touched, and her eyes swam with tears. Sterne was back and he was saying things she'd never dared hope to hear from him. And his next words sent her spinning.

"Will you marry me, Brynnie?" he asked huskily. "I know I don't deserve you, but I promise I'll always try to make you happy."

This heartfelt proposal was so different from the first uncertain one. She wrapped her arms around him and grinned with pure happiness. This time she knew he really meant it. She knew how much he loved her. "Oh, yes, Sterne, I'll marry you."

His whole face lighted with joy. He picked her up and carried her into the bedroom, and she snuggled deep in his arms, feeling feminine and cherished and loved. They came together in a shattering blaze of intensity that combined both tenderness and passion, binding them to each other, heart, body, and soul, forever.

They lay together, clinging to each other, for a long time afterward, not wanting to let go. "I got the sales agreement for the house from Ginger Stroud," Sterne said as he ran a lazy, possessive hand over her body, which was tucked into the curve of his. "And I'm sure I'm going to be accepted by every law school I apply to." He grinned. "I tell you, those places are celebrity-hungry."

"If you go to law school, you're going to do well, celebrity or not," Brynn said with loving firmness. "I'll make sure you study and take it seriously. Your days of coasting by on your name are over, Sterne Lipton."

"I know. Now I've got you to keep me in line." He smiled happily, obviously delighted at the prospect. Then he sobered, suddenly serious. "And I want you to be proud of me, Brynnie. I want to be the kind of man you want, the type of man you deserve. The type of man you can talk to and depend on. The type of man who is capable of sustaining a relationship with just one woman and making a commitment to her."

"The type of man who wants children someday," she finished softly, remembering that night in his car when she'd told Sterne her list of prerequisites in a mate. She was both astonished and moved that he'd remembered too.

"I want to be that man for you, Brynnie. And with you by my side, I know I can be."

"I know," she whispered, holding him close.

"I guess I'm just what you were looking for, after all." He sighed with contentment. "A nice, normal, marriageable man."

"Yes." She kissed him. "Definitely a marrying man."

THE EDITOR'S CORNER

Last month I briefly told you the good news that The Delaney Dynasty lives on! Next month you'll get a sneak preview of the second trio of Delaney books, **THE DELANEYS OF KILLAROO,** in a Free Sampler you'll see everywhere! It's part of a promotion that is unique in publishing history and is being done jointly by LOVESWEPT and Clairol®. In the late fall last year, a creative and effervescent young woman representing Clairol, Inc., came to see us at Bantam. Their market research had identified the "perfect user" of a new hair product they were developing as the same woman who reads LOVESWEPT romances! You, my friends out there, were described as intelligent, clever, fun loving, optimistic, romantic women who cared about and tried to make a contribution to family, friends, community, and country. Sounds right to me, I said. The new product from Clairol®—PAZAZZ® SHEER COLORWASH—is a continuation of the PAZAZZ® line of temporary (and, I must add, fun) coloring gels, mousses, and color wands. But what truly amazed me was that one of the colors they had "invented"—*Sheer Plum* —had just been "invented" by Fayrene Preston for her heroine Sydney in **THE DELANEYS OF KILLAROO**. Further, while Iris Johansen's and Kay Hooper's heroines weren't described in the precise terms of the new Clairol® colors, they were so close that one had to begin to believe that our two companies were fated to get together with **THE DELANEYS OF KILLAROO** and **PAZAZZ® SHEER COLOR-WASH**. So we decided to do a promotion featuring a Sampler of the new books about the Australian branch of the Delaney family, whose heroines had Sheer Colorwash hair colors. And in each Sampler Clairol® gives you a Beauty Bonus full of tips on hair beauty and styling using the new products. Next month at health and beauty aid sections of stores and at cosmetic counters you will find the Free Sampler. You'll also find the Free Samplers when you go to your local bookselling outlet. In all, more than three-quarters of a million copies of these Samplers will be given away during a six-week period. Then, when **THE DELANEYS OF KILLAROO** books are published in August, the first 200,000 copies of each title will carry a special money-saving coupon from Clairol® so that you—you "perfect users" you!—can try

(continued)

PAZAZZ® SHEER COLORWASH at a lower price. I hope you'll enjoy this promotion since you are its special focus. Lots of other women who may never have heard of LOVE-SWEPT romances will learn about them, too, as all of us learn for the first time about a brand-new way to put more PAZAZZ® into our lives with color highlights ranging from subtle to dramatic ... from the glints of gold in Sheer Cinnamon or Amber to the glow of a fine wine in Sheer Plum or Burgundy. We on the LOVESWEPT staff have been treated by Clairol® to samples of all these products ... and if you could see us now! We, in turn, treated the Clairol® ladies to the Delaney books and other LOVESWEPTs, and they loved them! We've had so much fun with this promotion, and we hope you, too, will enjoy this first-ever promotion with you in mind.

Now for a few words about the delightful LOVESWEPTs in store for you next month.

We are so pleased to introduce a wonderful new talent, Glenna McReynolds, making her debut as a published author with **SCOUT'S HONOR,** LOVESWEPT #198. In this charming love story Mitch Summers, a wonderfully masterful and yet vulnerable man, follows stunningly beautiful Anna Lange from San Francisco to the Bahamas to ask her a simple favor: would she turn her gambling skills on a cheating cardsharp and win back the land his brother lost in a crooked poker game? After a disastrous experience with a fortune hunter, Anna holds all men at arm's length, but she cannot resist Mitch's boyish charm ... or his passionate kisses. With the glamour of high stakes poker and with the heart-warming emotion of sensuous romance, this is a fabulous first love story from Glenna McReynolds.

Prepare to be glued to your chair, unable to put down **ALLURE,** LOVESWEPT #199, by Fayrene Preston. Breathtakingly passionate and emotional, **ALLURE** is the love story of Rick O'Neill and Chandra Stuart, star-crossed lovers who meet once more after years apart. Only Rick can't remember very much about Chandra, and she has never been able to forget a single thing about him! Then, haunted by a scent that brings along with it a powerful memory, Rick begins to unravel the mystery of the past ... and blaze a trail toward a future with the woman he loves. An enthralling, powerful romance.

(continued)

We are delighted to announce that Joan Bramsch—author of such wonderful, beloved LOVESWEPTs as **THE SOPHISTI-CATED MOUNTAIN GAL** and **THE STALLION MAN**—has the distinction of being the author of our two-hundredth LOVESWEPT, **WITH NO RESERVATIONS**! Hotel executive Ann Waverly is understandably intrigued by Jeffrey Madison. The first time she meets him he looks like something the cat dragged in; the second time, he's wearing only a sheet! Jeffrey is powerfully attracted to Ann, but his suspicious actions make her wary of him and the potent effect he has on her senses. Actually, both Ann and Jeffrey have their secrets, and you'll be kept on the edge of your seat as Joan skillfully weaves this tale of humor and deep love.

Linda Cajio gives us another lighthearted and touching romance with **RESCUING DIANA,** LOVESWEPT #201. At a reception Adam Roberts is captivated by Diana Windsor—nicknamed Princess Di—an endearingly innocent and shy creator of computer games. Diana is equally enchanted by Adam—he's her knight in shining armor come to life. But neither Adam nor Diana expected he would *really* have to rescue this princess from all sorts of modern-day dragons. As you follow Adam and Diana from one delightful escapade to another, you'll fall as much in love with them as they do with each other.

Enjoy!
Warm regards,

Carolyn Nichols

Carolyn Nichols
 Editor
LOVESWEPT
Bantam Books, Inc.
666 Fifth Avenue
New York, NY 10103

NEW!
Handsome Book Covers Specially Designed To Fit Loveswept Books

Our new French Calf Vinyl book covers come in a set of three great colors—royal blue, scarlet red and kachina green.

Each 7" × 9½" book cover has two deep vertical pockets, a handy sewn-in bookmark, and is soil and scratch resistant.

To order your set, use the form below.

The first Delaney trilogy

Heirs to a great dynasty, the Delaney brothers were united by blood, united by devotion to their rugged land . . . and known far and wide as

THE SHAMROCK TRINITY

Bantam's bestselling LOVESWEPT romance line built its reputation on quality and innovation. Now, a remarkable and unique event in romance publishing comes from the same source: THE SHAMROCK TRINITY, three daringly original novels written by three of the most successful women's romance writers today. Kay Hooper, Iris Johansen, and Fayrene Preston have created a trio of books that are dynamite love stories bursting with strong, fascinating male and female characters, deeply sensual love scenes, the humor for which LOVESWEPT is famous, and a deliciously fresh approach to romance writing.

THE SHAMROCK TRINITY—Burke, York, and Rafe: Powerful men . . . rakes and charmers . . . they needed only love to make their lives complete.

☐ *RAFE, THE MAVERICK by Kay Hooper*

Rafe Delaney was a heartbreaker whose ebony eyes held laughing devils and whose lilting voice could charm any lady—or any horse—until a stallion named Diablo left him in the dust. It took Maggie O'Riley to work her magic on the impossible horse . . . and on his bold owner. Maggie's grace and strength made Rafe yearn to share the raw beauty of his land with her, to teach her the exquisite pleasure of yielding to the heat inside her. Maggie was stirred by Rafe's passion, but would his reputation and her ambition keep their kindred spirits apart?   (21846 • $2.75)

LOVESWEPT

☐ *YORK, THE RENEGADE by Iris Johansen*

Some men were made to fight dragons, Sierra Smith thought when she first met York Delaney. The rebel brother had roamed the world for years before calling the rough mining town of Hell's Bluff home. Now, the spirited young woman who'd penetrated this renegade's paradise had awakened a savage and tender possessiveness in York: something he never expected to find in himself. Sierra had known loneliness and isolation too—enough to realize that York's restlessness had only to do with finding a place to belong. Could she convince him that love was such a place, that the refuge he'd always sought was in her arms?

(21847 • $2.75)

☐ *BURKE, THE KINGPIN by Fayrene Preston*

Cara Winston appeared as a fantasy, racing on horseback to catch the day's last light—her silver hair glistening, her dress the color of the Arizona sunset . . . and Burke Delaney wanted her. She was on his horse, on his land: she would have to belong to him too. But Cara was quicksilver, impossible to hold, a wild creature whose scent was midnight flowers and sweet grass. Burke had always taken what he wanted, by willing it or fighting for it; Cara cherished her freedom and refused to believe his love would last. Could he make her see he'd captured her to have and hold forever?

(21848 • $2.75)